I pressed my face into the kitchen window. I looked right and left, but I didn't see him. And when I turned from the window, thinking that whatever he was doing was his business, anyway, I saw him at the screen door, his hand raised, fist clenched, ready to knock. He knocked once on the screen door, opened it, knocked again on the inside door, saw me through its window, opened the door, and came in.

"Hi," I said. "What's up?"

He nodded, again stiffly, to indicate the area he'd been working in. "I dug up somethin' out there," he said.

"Oh?" I said.

"Yeah. I dug up an arm. I dug up someone's arm."

THE PEOPLE OF THE DARK

Look for these other TOR books by T. M. Wright

CARLISLE STREET
A MANHATTAN GHOST STORY
THE PLAYGROUND

THE PEOPLE OF THE DARK

T. M. WRIGHT

TOR

A TOM DOHERTY ASSOCIATES BOOK

DEDICATION
With love, for Chris

THE PEOPLE OF THE DARK

Copyright © 1985 by T. M. Wright

First printing: March 1985

A TOR Book

Published by Tom Doherty Associates
8-10 West 36 Street
New York, N.Y. 10018

ISBN: 0-812-52752-6
CAN. ED.: 0-812-52753-4

Printed in the United States of America

When I was a boy of eleven or twelve I was walking alone at dusk through a heavily wooded park near my home. It was a park I'd walked through almost every evening on my way home from school and I felt at ease in it, even when the light was failing and the whisper of an evening chill was in the air. Above the hulking, dark and ragged line of the trees, the sky always had the pale yellow glow of the city splattered on it, and every now and then I could hear the blare of a car horn, or a dog barking, or, depending on if I was near the perimeter of the park, a family argument erupting out of nowhere. These were comforting sights and sounds because they told me that civilization was close by, that I was not alone, after all, though, if I wanted, I could *pretend* that I was alone. And that was something I pretended quite a lot. Because being alone, in the woods, in the dark, was spooky, and spooky was fun.

That's what I was doing that night when I was eleven or twelve, and coming home through the park at dusk. I was pretending that I was alone, that the park was a vast and uncorrupted wilderness, that there were no houses within shouting distance, and no city lights painting the dusk a grimy yellow. I was pretending that there were bears close by, and bobcats, foxes, moose, rattlesnakes. I was transporting myself to a place where the earth itself was not just many things—friend, enemy, mother—it was the *only* thing.

And on that particular early evening when I was eleven or twelve, I sat down in a clearing surrounded by evergreens and thickets to watch the night come. I remember I was hungry because the lunch that day in school had been something awful—peanut butter sandwiches on Wonderbread, with carrot salad as a side dish—so I'd skipped it. And, as well, the beginnings of a cold were moving about in my blood. But I was something of a dreamer, and I was young, so there was very little that could stop me from doing what I wanted to do.

It was a Friday; I had that small and special kind of happiness that comes only to schoolkids on Fridays, when two whole days of freedom have opened up before them. And I remember that it was early in the school year, September, probably, because the evening was warm, and humid; I could hear mosquitoes whining in the air around me, and that got me to thinking that the bats soon would come to eat them. I didn't like bats, but the idea that soon they'd be silently scooping up their evening meal in the air above me gave me only a passing shiver.

That particular clearing was one I'd paused in a couple of dozen times before. It was rimmed by tall evergreens, a few venerable old maples, and one immense and dying oak whose branches already were nearly bare of leaves.

It was from behind the dark trunk of that oak— visible only as a patchy, black *presence* against the backdrop of gathering darkness— that a child appeared and swept toward me with his arms wide and, when he was only a couple of feet away, and I could see him more clearly, a look of immense desperation and pleading on his face. Then he was gone.

STRANGE SEED

Realization, like punishment, comes swiftly to the child. And, as to punishment, he winces and stifles a moan. Here, in the bright sunlight, denial is impossible. He sees that his father's body is becoming what swamps are made of, and soil is made of—becoming food for the horsetail, and clover, and burying beetles, and a million others. Because the earth, the breathing earth, must be constantly nourished.

His father's words are closer now, and understandable. "Decay is not the grim thing it appears to be. It is renewal."

"Father?" the child pleads, realizing the futility of the word. "Father?" he repeats, more in memory of those times his father responded to the word than for any other reason.

Father?—distantly, from the thickets to the south. *Father?* Barely audible.

The child looks questioningly up from his father's body. "Father?" he calls.

Father?

An echo, the child thinks. Months before, he remembers, in the heart of the forest, "Hello," extended, "Hello," repeated, "Hello," shouted back at both of them, father and son, by the voices of the forest.

"Hello," the child calls.

Father? replies the voice of the thickets.

"Hello," the child calls. And distantly, from the east, from the forest, "Hello, Hello, Hello," decreasing in intensity. And finally, nothing.

Hello—from the thickets.

"Hello," the child calls.

Hello.

"Hello, Father!" the child calls.

And the forest replies, "Hello, Father! Hello, Father!"

And the voice of the thickets replies, *Hello, Father! Father? Hello!*

NURSERY TALE

The first three young couples in Granada—the Meades, the McIntyres, the Wentises—were very much of a type, it was true. Bright young suburbanites with a taste for getting ahead, who liked being looked upon as "special," but who tried, to varying degrees, to carry that perception of status with humility. They all gave generously to the proper charities, they all belonged to one of the two major political parties, the men all held white-collar jobs. Which is not to say that these couples were indistinguishable, one from another. . . .

The McIntyres, the Meades, and the Wentises came to Granada in pursuit of a dream. They believed what the brochure had told them about "open spaces and room to breathe—all within the framework of a secure, planned community" because that was what modern living was all about. It was their birthright, wasn't it, to seek out what was most comfortable, and easy.

That was the dream, after all.

And all of them were dreamers.

THE CHILDREN OF THE ISLAND

And on the Upper West Side, in a law office on West 110th Street, the newly installed junior partner of the law firm of Johnson, Bigny and Belles, a young woman named Karen Gears looked up from her work at a window which faced south and one word escaped her, "No!" It was a plea, a word of desperation—keep the dreams away, lock them up in her childhood, where they belonged, where, indeed, they had begun, and where she had supposed they had ended. . . .

On the fringes of the West Village, in lower Manhattan, a good-looking, dark-haired, gray-eyed boy was lying on his back on his bed. The lights were out, the shades and curtains drawn. He had always liked darkness.

He was remembering that just two days before, he had somehow gotten Christine Basile, of all people, to agree to go out with him. He was remembering, also, that barely a month before, he'd celebrated a birthday. His sixteenth, he'd been told. The man who called himself his father had given him an extra set of keys to the car.

The boy was weeping now, and he was whispering to himself, "What a crock of shit, what a damned crock of shit!" . . .

In Manhattan, on West Tenth Street, in a small bachelor apartment which had been decorated very tastefully in earth tones, and included a wicker loveseat, bamboo shades, and a large, well-maintained freshwater aquarium, a man named Philip Case—who was apparently in his early thirties—was holding his head and tightly gritting his teeth, trying futilely to shut out the images that came to him in waves, like a tide filled with bad memories. . . .

There were a hundred or more Philip Cases in Manhattan that night. A hundred or more Karen Gears. A hundred or more boys lying in their darkened rooms and trying desperately to recall the events of just one or two days before. Because such events were their reality, and reality was rapidly slipping away from them. . . .

They had become what they had lived amongst. They had grown apart from the earth, because they had rarely touched it.

They had grown secure in what they'd become, and so had tossed aside what they had been. In stark desperation they had discarded it, and forgotten it. Because it was impossible to be both what they were, and what they had changed themselves into.

I have snapshots of Erika when she was a child. Most of them are in black and white, though some are in color, and I say to myself when I look at them, *Yes, I can see the woman here, in this child; she hasn't changed much. Her face got a little narrower, perhaps—she grew taller, her body matured. But the woman dwelt there.* I think it's a comfortable lie to tell myself, though I'm not sure that it is a lie. If it is, I want desperately to believe it.

One of these photographs, one in black and white, shows Erika at what appears to be the age of ten or eleven. She's standing with her left arm around a boy who's about the same age; his name, she says, was Timothy. He could easily have been her twin. They were about the same height; both had dark hair and darkish skin, and they shared the same pixieish look, as if they had wings on their backs.

"What happened to him?" I asked her once.

She shrugged. "What happens to anyone, Jack? He grew up, he got married. I think he's a plumber; maybe he's an electrician. I haven't seen him in years."

Another of the photographs shows Erika and her mother cheek to cheek. The photograph was obviously taken in one of those booths where a series of black-and-white shots can be had for a dollar or two. Erika's mother is smiling broadly, and Erika is smiling broadly, though her face is blurred a little, as if she turned her head when the shutter clicked. She told me she was fourteen when the photograph was taken, and that her mother died a month later—"It was a car crash, Jack. My father died too. They're buried together." She smiled, embarrassed. "Well, not together, really. Side by side."

I have several baby pictures of Erika. One is an 8 × 10 color portrait done at Sears, another is a small snapshot commemorating her first visit to the beach: She's sitting in a tiny, two-ring inflatable pool; an adult's arm is jutting in from the left side of the snapshot, the hand apparently on her back, holding her up in the pool. The beach is behind her.

* * *

Erika is twenty-six years old, short, dark-skinned, dark-haired. Her eyes are very large and are a rich, earthy brown in color. Her face is oval, her nose small and straight, her lips full. It is a memorable face not only because it is so marvelous to look at but also because it has something undefinable in it, as if the brain behind it is holding onto knowledge or memory that it must desperately keep to itself. That's why she often looks bemused, I think.

She tells jokes on occasion. Some of them are dirty and some of them are clean, and some of them display an incredible naiveté, as if she has, as an adult, just discovered jokes that were extant when the rest of us were children. "I'm going to make rice and updoc for dinner, Jack," she said once.

"You're going to make what?" I asked.

"Rice and updoc," she repeated.

So I fell for it. "What's updoc?" I said, which elicited a full minute of wonderful childlike laughter from her.

She has no brothers or sisters. She remembers her parents were anguished over that because they very much wanted other children. "They kept trying, Jack," she told me. "And it wasn't that my mother couldn't get pregnant. She could. She got pregnant a half-dozen times anyway. The trouble was, she miscarried a half-dozen times, too." Erika has told me that more than once, always in the same words. And she always adds, her voice low and thoughtful, "It's really too bad, isn't it? I would like to have had some brothers and sisters. I think my childhood would

seem fuller if I'd had some brothers and sisters."
She pauses, looks quizzically at me. "I remember so
awfully little from my childhood, Jack. Is it that way
with you?"

I tell her, "Sure it is. I think it's that way
with everyone," which is a lie, of course.

Erika and I have been married for six years. It's
the first marriage for both of us, and we went into it
good and starry-eyed; we would have looked just like
the bride and groom on a wedding cake had we had a
traditional ceremony, but we didn't. We were married at a place called Sonnenburg Gardens, in
Canandaigua, New York. It's a sprawling three-story
mansion with a red-slate roof, and it's surrounded by
thirty acres of meticulously cared-for gardens. Erika
loved it—I thought it was okay, if a bit overstylized—
and when she learned that marriages could be per-
formed there, she was ecstatic.

She loves to get her hands into the earth, loves the
smell of it, the texture of it. And she loves the things
that spring from the earth; she says she feels a kin-
ship with them. I tell her I do too, and that's the
truth. But I know she means something deeper than I
mean. I know that now, especially.

She wears no perfume. She has a smell all her
own, which is vaguely, and faintly, like the smell of
sweet butter. It's especially noticeable when we make
love. I think it's in her sweat, and I enjoy it because,
of course, it reminds me of her. It lingers. It's on

her clothes; it's on the chair she uses most often. It fades after a time. Then her clothes and her favorite chair become simple and inanimate and uninteresting.

It's in the walls, too, where it's extremely tenacious. And it's in the garden she started. And when I smell it here and there on our land, I stop and I enjoy it.

She looks especially good in blue and in green, which complement her dark hair, darkish skin, and brown eyes.

She likes ginger ale, black coffee, tuna fish on whole wheat, Humphrey Bogart movies, most of Woody Allen, none of Sidney Sheldon.

And she scares easily, laughs a lot, is afraid of the dark, likes to be hugged, wears comfortable shoes, is a sucker for a salesman, dynamite in a bathing suit, allergic to penicillin.

I am happy with her. I'll always be happy with her.

Book One

CHAPTER ONE

When Erika and I moved into our farmhouse, we knew that there was a leak where the line from the well—seven hundred feet up what we used to call "our mountain"—entered the basement. We were told by a local contractor that the leak was caused by an underground stream and that the only way to fix it would be to have a trench dug around the perimeter of the house, then to have the trench lined with ceramic tile and PVC pipe. He said it would divert the stream, and we said okay.

He subcontracted the job to a man named Jim Sandy,

who came to the house on a bright and unusually warm afternoon early in December, took himself on a quick walking tour of the area he was going to be digging up, then came back into the house to give me an estimate. I showed him to the kitchen, sat him down at the table, made him some coffee. He put lots of sugar in it, then sipped it delicately.

I sat kitty-corner to him at the table, with my own coffee. "What's the verdict?" I said.

"Lots of rocks in there," he said. "Rocks and hard clay. It's damn difficult to dig through rocks and hard clay."

"Yes," I said. "I imagine it is."

"Five hundred dollars," he said. He was a short, thin man, with grayish skin and bad teeth. He was wearing a threadbare blue denim jacket, a red flannel shirt, black pants, Timberland boots, and an oil-stained orange cap with the word CHALMERS imprinted on it.

"Five hundred dollars is a lot of money," I told him.

"You get what you pay for," he said, which surprised me—I had supposed, from looking at him, that he'd haggle. He took another sip of coffee, a noisy one, and repeated, "You get what you pay for."

He smelled vaguely of wood smoke thickly overlaid by a cheap after-shave that I supposed he'd splashed on to cover the odor of the wood smoke. Whenever he put his cup of coffee down, he scratched idly at the inside of his elbow and cursed beneath his breath.

"How about three hundred?" I said.

He grinned, took another sip of coffee, set the cup down. "Three hundred'll get me here," he said, still grinning. "And five hundred'll get the job done."

I thought a moment, then shrugged. "Okay," I said.

He scratched his elbow, cursed, shook my hand firmly, and told me he'd be back a week later. He said that the job would take a full day.

The farmhouse Erika and I bought had been on the market for nearly two years, so we got it cheap. It's old but solid, and was completely renovated ten years ago. It has a new black tile roof, new aluminum siding (a light aquamarine that blends well with the evergreens, maples, and walnut trees around the house), and someone had once even made an attempt at landscaping, though what remained of that attempt when we got here was only a line of uncared-for privet hedges alongside the driveway and a wide circle of bricks just to the south of the house, with a fieldstone walkway leading from it.

The house sits three hundred feet back from the road, at the crest of a small hill. Our "mountain"—all one hundred and fifty acres of it—looms behind the house. This is the Finger Lakes Region of New York, fifty miles or so from the Pennsylvania line, so what we call a mountain is actually no more than a steep hill littered with dead trees and eroding fast. The real estate agent told us, "The land is useless, of course," and we told him that that was okay, that we'd have privacy, at least.

There are two other dwellings on our one hundred and fifty acres. One is just a stone foundation with some uprights remaining from the original frame. The other is a sad, three-room log cabin whose walls tilt and tar-paper roof sags precariously. It sits in a small clearing a thousand feet north of the house, also at the base of our mountain, so it's level with the house. It's just far enough from the house that hunters can sit in it unnoticed and wait for deer or opossums or raccoons to wander by. Erika and I discussed getting a permit to burn the place down, but it was an idea that never got beyond the talking stages.

Erika and I are good together. We get a kick out of pretty much the same things; our sex life is usually exciting ("Our bodies fit together nicely," we say), and for six years we've been very happy. We have had our ups and downs, of course. Everyone does.

She's left me several times. Not for other men. Other relationships never seemed to be a problem for us (she *looks* at other men, of course, and I at other women, and we often like what we see, but it's never threatened to go further than that for me, and I think for her, too). She's left me because of her *ideas*. She left me once, for instance, to go live with a cult that had cut off contact with society, much as the Shakers did, in Pennsylvania, but the group that Erika got involved with did it much more completely, with a great deal more gusto and cynicism. And that, I believe, is what finally drove her from them—that constant loud aura of superiority, the idea that because they were *apart* from society and were living according to their own rules and their own ideas, they were, of course, somehow *above* society.

She was gone for two months, and although I knew where she was—she'd left me a letter—I realized it was something she'd have to work out for herself. And when she got back and we were talking about the whole thing, she told me, "We all come from the same mother, don't we, Jack? No one can deny that. *They* certainly can't deny that." I agreed, though the remark mystified me, then. It doesn't, now.

And another time she left, for not quite as long, for a religious group that had developed what they called "A Live-in College for the Spiritually Enlightened" in the Berkshires, in New Hampshire. It wasn't a typical college, of course. It was a very large and pitifully ramshackle farmhouse that the group—which totaled about sixty men and women, ranging from sixteen to eighty years of age—had covered with a coat of light lavender paint. A large, rectangular sign over the front doors read, in lavender on a white background, GOD LOVES YOU—PASS IT ON. Below that, in simple black block letters, COLLEGE FOR THE SPIRITUALLY ENLIGHTENED. When Erika came back after that encounter, she was confused.

"Who has to *go* anywhere, Jack? I don't understand that. No one has to go anywhere."

"They're going somewhere, Erika?" I asked.

"Sure. They say they're going to heaven. They

say they're going to be with God. And I don't understand. No one has to *go* anywhere for that.''

She is short—about five feet five—dark, curvaceous, and very smart. She used to say now and then, "You still think you're smarter than I am, don't you?" And I used to shake my head glumly and admit that I wasn't. She never believed me; she always thought I was humoring her.

She was the one who made the decision to buy the farmhouse. A week after seeing the house, we were watching reruns of *The Good Neighbors* on TV, and she said, without looking at me, "I want to buy that house, Jack.''

"Which one?" I asked. We'd looked at six or seven houses in the past couple of weeks.

"That big farmhouse," she answered. "The one with the privet hedge.''

"Oh," I said. "Why?''

"Because I think it's charming," she answered, and she glanced quickly at me, smiled, added, "And I think we can be happy there.''

"Aren't we happy here?" *Here* was a townhouse apartment just south of Syracuse, New York.

"*Happier*, there," she said.

We moved in a month and a half later. Jim Sandy came over with his backhoe to dig a trench and lay ceramic tile and PVC pipe two weeks after that.

Erika was in the city that day, working. She owned a small record shop that kept her away from home quite a lot because she was devoted to it and felt that with enough devotion it might make a good deal of money someday.

I watched as Jim Sandy towed his backhoe up the long, steep driveway, started it, unloaded it. I expected that he'd come and announce himself, but he didn't. He chugged around to the side of the house, the treads of the backhoe chewing up the lawn and spitting out huge divots. Then, with a great thud, the shovel sank into the earth and he started to work. From a kitchen window, I watched him for a few minutes. He looked at me once; I smiled and waved at him. He nodded stiffly from the cab of the backhoe. It made me feel instantly that, even from behind the window, I was somehow in his way, so I busied myself with some unpacking and listened to the grinding chugga-chugga of the backhoe.

That chugga-chugga stopped a half hour or so after it started. I waited for it to start again, and when, after a few minutes, it didn't, I went to the kitchen window and looked out. The backhoe was a good fifty feet from where it had been a half hour earlier, and its shovel was stuck into the earth. I didn't see Jim Sandy and decided that he'd probably had to relieve himself and felt more comfortable behind a tree or the garage.

I pressed my face into the kitchen window. I looked right and left, but I didn't see him. And when I turned from the window, thinking that whatever he was doing was his business, anyway, I saw him at the screen door, his hand raised, fist clenched, ready to knock. He knocked once on the screen door, opened it, knocked again on the inside door, saw me through its window, opened the door, and came in.

"Hi," I said. "What's up?"

He nodded, again stiffly, to indicate the area he'd been working in. "I dug up somethin' out there," he said.

"Oh?" I said.

"Yeah. I dug up an arm. I dug up someone's arm."

CHAPTER TWO

Erika screwed her face up and said, "That's disgusting, Jack. Did you *look* at it?"

"Sure I did," I told her. "Why not?"

"What did it look like?" she asked. "Was it a skeleton? Was it just bones?"

"Mostly," I said. "There was some skin attached to it. It looked like a rolled-up grocery bag, Erika. There was nothing *upsetting* about it."

"And was there anything else?" Now, her look of disgust was mixed with curiosity.

"Anything else?"

"Sure. You find an arm and you'll probably find . . . other things."

"Nothing yet, Erika."

She rolled her eyes. "That's comforting."

"This bothers you, doesn't it?" I said.

"Huh?" she said, clearly incredulous.

"I asked if this bothered you." I paused very briefly. "I guess it probably does."

She reached up and patted the top of my head. "Yes, Jack," she said. "It bothers me."

I felt very foolish.

She had an accident once that scared the hell out of me. She was cleaning the cellar floor of our townhouse in Syracuse. It was particularly dirty because we'd been gone for a week and a half, and our cats' litter box had grown too filthy for them, so they'd started using the floor. The smell was awful.

I was upstairs, making dinner, when the accident happened. She'd been moving some aluminum screens and windows that had been leaning against the wall—the cats had utilized the area behind these screens and windows—when one of the windows shattered. A shard of glass put a nasty gash in her arm, just above the wrist, and when I got down there, after hearing her scream, I found her holding the arm tightly, eyes wide, mouth open. I realized she was going into shock.

The gash was bleeding badly; my first thought was that an artery had been severed, so I led her to the cellar steps, sat her down, ran upstairs and grabbed a dishtowel, ran back, and made a tourniquet.

"I'm taking you to the emergency room, Erika."

She shook her head.

"Erika, this is a very *bad* wound; you might have severed an artery."

She shook her head again. "No," she whispered.

"You're being stubborn."

"I'm not," she managed. "The bleeding will stop, Jack." She sounded very sure of herself. "It's not bad."

I believed her. I told myself that I was being foolish. "Yeah, and where'd you get your medical degree?"

And she said, with that same stiff self-confidence, "I know my body, Jack."

I sat beside her. I saw that much of the towel, which was white, had turned a deep shade of red. "What were you doing, Erika?" I asked, merely for something to say.

"I was moving one of those windows, Jack. The cats crapped behind it."

"This is foolish," I began, and she interrupted, "I know my body, Jack."

I was nervous, of course; I nearly said something suggestive, something to lighten the tension between us. Instead I asked, "Am I being overly protective?"

"Yes. But it's okay. The bleeding has stopped."

I shook my head. She took the towel off her arm. The bleeding had indeed stopped. I shook my head again. "Keep it wrapped up, Erika, please—"

"No," she said. "It's okay."

And it was. A narrow, almost invisible scar is all that remains.

*   *   *

Several days after Jim Sandy's discovery I told her, "Jim Sandy said that other . . . body parts have been found in the area."

We were in bed. I felt her stiffen up beside me; she said nothing for a few moments. Then: "On our property, you mean?"

"I think so. I'd have to check."

"Check what?"

"The survey map. I'd have to pace the boundary out, I think. What does it matter?"

"It matters," she said, her tone very earnest. "I don't care if they find 'body parts' somewhere else, Jack. It's no concern of mine. But when they start finding them on *my* property—" She paused. When she continued, her tone was softer. "It's spooky, Jack."

"It gives the place atmosphere," I said.

She said nothing.

"Don't you think it gives the place atmosphere, Erika?"

"No," she whispered.

"Do you think we should move?"

"Not yet," she said.

"When, then?"

"When they start finding heads and torsos and thighs and eyeballs and . . ." She paused. "*Then* we move!"

"It's a deal," I said.

But we never moved from the house. In retrospect, maybe we should have. It probably wouldn't have made any difference, after all, but the effort might have given me some brief comfort.

I'm a commercial artist. In college I studied fine arts—it's what I got my master's in, in fact—and I had grand ideas of making some kind of living as a painter. I didn't care if it was a good living, or even a poor one. I was willing to suffer. I did suffer. For ten years, I went from one lousy job to another—I laid sewer pipe; I washed dishes; I was a gardener's helper, a carpenter's helper, a plumber's assistant. And all the while I told myself, and believed it, that I was doing it "for the sake of art." I did hundreds of paintings. Landscapes, mostly, and a few dozen portraits (when friends or relatives pleaded with me to do something with my painting that would get me some *money*). I sold five of the landscapes in ten years (earning a total of $825.00 from them), and all of the portraits, because they were, in a sense, commissioned. And one morning, seven years ago, I sliced my face up while shaving with a razor blade that should have been replaced weeks earlier, but I literally did not have the money to replace it. I looked at myself in the mirror and whispered, "Enough! This has gone far enough!" A week later I had a position as an apprentice commercial artist with an ad agency in Elmira, New York.

I was still working for that agency when Erika and I bought the farmhouse. The agency had moved to Syracuse, a good 125 miles from the house, but they trusted me to do much of my work at home, so it wasn't a matter of commuting that distance every day. Once or twice a week would do it.

My work is fairly well known. I've done jobs for Coca-Cola, for Pampers, for IBM, and NIKON, and Burpee Seeds, plus several dozen others. No one knows that the work they're looking at is mine, although I've managed to slip my initials into a few ads (check the rectangular reflection of white light on the Coca-Cola ads that feature a koala bear). I've resigned myself to anonymity.

Jim Sandy never finished his trench. He came back to the house the day after he'd begun work and told me, "Sorry, Mr. Harris, but you gotta get yourself someone else to do this work."

"Who, for instance?" I asked.

He shrugged. "Beats me." Then he loaded up his backhoe and left. I think the cellar leaks to this day.

Life at the farmhouse was going to be rustic, I realized. We had no trash pickup, for instance. We got a permit from the town clerk that allowed us to use a sanitary landfill three miles east of the village. This weekly job started shortly after we moved to the house. We put a half-dozen plastic bags filled with trash and garbage into my Toyota and carted the whole stinking mess to the landfill, which, we found, was down a half-dozen narrow dirt roads. It gave us a chance to scout out the area, anyway, which Erika enjoyed. There were a lot of mobile homes, most of them with makeshift tile roofs—I guessed that it was a town zoning ordinance—a trailer looked less like a trailer and was indeed more stationary and therefore a more permanent part of the tax base if it had an extra roof on it. There were also several small, crudely built houses, some with tarpaper roofs and windows covered with plastic—most apparently had fallen into years of disuse. A few were inhabited. We saw several scruffy children standing around, looking bored, their equally bored-looking mothers behind them; this bothered Erika a lot. She said that children who had to be so close to the earth should learn to enjoy it. I accused her of naiveté, and the subject was dropped.

We saw a couple of joggers, too, which I didn't expect. I had assumed that jogging was an urban pastime and that rural people did enough hard work that jogging was unnecessary. "You're a snob," Erika said, and I agreed.

"These people do seem to put more into it, though," I said. And it was true. One of the joggers, a man apparently in his late thirties, legs and arms and chest well-muscled, head bobbing, dark hair flying this way and that, looked wonderfully involved in what he was doing.

"Now that man's *serious* about it, Erika," I said. "He's not just fooling around."

"Of course he's not fooling around," she said. "He obviously knows the value of what he's got."

"The value of what he's got?" I asked.

She nodded. "Yes. His body. He knows how

precious it is." She gave me a quick once over, reached and patted my stomach. "You could use a little *self-appreciation* yourself, Jack."

I glanced at her, grinned. "Oh? I thought you liked that . . ."—I looked down briefly at the slight protrusion of my belly—"that small proof of my imperfection."

She laughed quickly. "Jack, I love what makes you human. I wouldn't change any of it." She patted my stomach again. "Even that."

"Thanks," I said, grinning. I glanced in the rearview mirror; the jogger had fallen. I stopped, looked back; Erika looked, too.

"He'll be okay," she said, an edge to her tone that surprised me.

I started backing up; the jogger was lying motionless face down in the road, his arms wide and his legs straight.

"Jack," Erika said sharply, "he doesn't *need* your help. He'll be *all right*."

I looked at her, surprised: "What are you saying, Erika?—'Don't get involved'?"

"Oh, of course not!" She was angry, now; I had rarely seen her so quick-tempered.

The jogger pushed his upper body off the road, then, as if he were doing pushups. I stopped the car, watched him bring his knees forward so he was on his haunches, take a long, deep breath, and stand.

Erika said, "These people can take care of them —*selves*, Jack, you'll see."

"Thanks," I said testily, "for you old-time country wisdom."

She sighed. "I'm sorry. I didn't mean to get angry with you." She reached, patted my belly yet again in an effort to lighten things up. "C'mon, let's go home and make love, paunch and all."

The area around the house is starkly rural. The road in front of it is paved but badly rutted, and our nearest neighbors, when we moved in, were an old German couple named Alnor who lived in a huge and immaculate white Victorian house a good mile and a half north of our house. The Alnors ran an antique shop in their small white barn, and we soon found that they were friendly enough if we looked to be on the verge of buying something, but became stiff and cool if we just wanted to talk. We never got to know them well. When the trouble started, they didn't come to us for help; they toughed it out for a while, all by themselves (I give them credit for that). Then one day I saw that their house had a FOR SALE BY OWNER sign stuck on it and a distinct air of abandonment about it.

The nearest town is called Cohocton. Once a year the locals stage what they call the Great Cohocton Tree-Sitting Festival, which involves neither trees nor sitting. Local men stand for twenty-four hours at a time on small platforms at the top of fifty-foot tall wooden poles. Lots of beer and handicrafts are sold at these festivals, and everyone involved seems to realize the kind of gritty charm they hold for city people, which Erika and I were. We've attended the Great Cohocton Tree-Sitting Festival only once, shortly after moving into the farmhouse. It was a sublimely simple diversion from the confusion of moving in and getting things straightened around. The men on the poles wore broad, clownlike smiles, as if they realized the idiocy of the whole event. There was no real purpose to it. No one won anything for the longest time standing on a pole. It was merely something pointless to do, and even more pointless to watch, and everyone enjoyed the hell out of it.

It wasn't until several days after Jim Sandy left with his backhoe that Erika asked me, "What kind of body parts, Jack?"

She was feeding our two cats their once-a-day can of Goff Pure Horsemeat Catfood (I'd once done some very good work for Goff, and as a kind of spiff they'd given me several years' worth of their cat food), and the kitchen smelled bad. "It's a hell of a time to ask something like that," I said.

She shrugged. "What's a good time?"

I shrugged, said, "None, I guess," paused, went on, "An arm. Some fingers. A few ribs."

"Where?"

"Where what?—Where'd they find the ribs?"

"No. Everything, Jack." Our cats—a wiry tom we called Orphan, because that's the way he came to us, and a big, orange longhair named Ginger—were rubbing against her ankles, now, telling her thank you, could they please have some more. "Where'd they find the other arm, and the fingers, and the ribs." She leaned over, stroked Ginger, said to her, "No, that's enough."

"Various places," I said. "Here and there. They found part of a head, too. Did I tell you that?"

That was a bombshell. Her mouth dropped open, though very briefly; she closed it at once, leaned over again, patted Ginger, said "No!" to her again.

"Did you hear what I said, Erika?"

She looked up at me. "I heard."

"And?"

She looked down at Ginger again. She said nothing.

"And?" I said again.

She shrugged, her head still lowered. "I don't know." She was clearly upset; her voice was trembling. "Fingers and toes I can deal with, Jack." A nervous smile flickered across her lips. " 'Part of a head' —that's a different story, isn't it?" She straightened, looked very seriously at me. "Isn't it?" she repeated.

"It was a very small part, I'm told," I said. "Part of a forehead, and part of a nose—they were attached—"

She cut in, "Oh, give me a break, Jack! I really don't want to hear this!" And she stalked from the room.

The boy who swept toward me from behind that dying oak twenty years ago was a boy I recognized. His name was Harry Simms. He was my age; we went to school together, we even shared some of the same classes. Earlier in the day, we'd been on opposite teams in a game of battle ball. Battle ball was a game we all liked because it allowed us to vent whatever pubescent anger and tension had built up—I think it gave us nearly the same kind of relief as masturbation.

He screamed this as he swept toward me from behind that oak: ''I can't breathe! I can't breathe!'' Then he was gone.

In school three days later, Harry's seat was empty and rumor had it that he'd run away from home. On my way back from school that night, through the park, I went looking for him.

CHAPTER THREE

The farmhouse has thirteen rooms, including five bedrooms, a huge dining room, a library, powder room, music room, formal living room, and at the rear, facing our mountain, a good-sized spare room that Erika and I use as a storage area. The house's previous owner, a retired Kodak executive in his late sixties, had begun to renovate this room. He'd put fake wooden beams in the ceiling and had laid a blue-speckled no-wax floor, but death caught up with him before the job was done. The walls were a scarred and patchy yellow-with-age plaster; here and there, he'd started to take the plaster down altogether, and diagonal gray wooden furring strips were visible beneath.

The room has a constant smell of fish to it. The smell varies in intensity from day to day—it seems to depend on the outside temperature and humidity. Erika and I decided that some hapless animal had crawled into the wall to die and that when we got around to finishing the job the Kodak executive had begun, we'd find the animal and give it a decent burial.

There were lots of small jobs to do at the house. The dining room needed painting; its teardrop crystal chandelier needed rewiring; several of the doors had to be rehung; a gutter on the northeast wall had to be replaced; a little bridge spanning a creek a hundred feet south of the house was in desperate need of rebuilding. We looked forward to seeing these jobs done. We were going to do them together. It was our first house, and we planned on being happy in it.

Of course, Jim Sandy's discovery got us off to a lousy start. I had hoped that it was the kind of thing that was so bizarre and so hard to believe that we could subconsciously deny it, that we'd be able to say to ourselves something like, *How could anyone find a man's arm in our side yard? How could anyone lose one?* And for a while that was precisely the attitude we were able to take. But at the same time that we asked the question we were able to answer it: "Yes, but it happened." And try as we might, we could not deny that. It happened. It was real.

I've lived in a few places since college: Baltimore; Syracuse; Rochester; Palmyra, New York (where Mormonism was founded); Harrisburg, Pennsylvania; and Dallas for a few weeks. I dearly love discovering a place I've moved to because all places are different. Two small towns within minutes of each other can be vastly different. And it's not just the people, though people are, of course, what make up a town and give it flavor. A valley town like Cohocton can be quite different from a hill town like Wayland or Dansville. Maybe because different kinds of people like to live in different kinds of places. Or maybe because the *place* molds its *people*.

So I looked forward to discovering what Cohocton was all about, to meeting its people, to finding out what their concerns were; I looked forward to seeing just what kind of life they'd made for themselves, to discovering the best roads to here and there, to finding landmarks along the way (an ancient barn with a tobacco ad on one wall, for instance, or a particularly old and gnarled oak tree, or an ancient, tumbledown farmhouse stuck by itself in the middle of a field lying fallow).

Some of this sense of discovery had to do with one of the ad campaigns I was working on then. It was for a company called Earth's-Way, a vitamin and mineral supplement manufacturer. They'd given me all the slogans—I could choose "Earth's Best" or "The Best from the Earth to You" or "The Best from the Earth's Kitchen to Your Table" or "From the Earth's Kitchen to You" or "The Best From the

Earth's Kitchen.'' There were others, and they all had to do with the fact that the company's products were ''one-hundred-percent natural and wholesome,'' a phrase that I had to work into the art. Some of the slogans were good, some were awful, and I was even given leeway to come up with something of my own, though I explained that I was strictly an artist, not a writer (although I think that it doesn't really take a writer to come up with a dynamite slogan; it takes a *salesman* with an ear for meter, and a jaded sense of the poetic).

So, my tours of discovery in and around Cohocton would probably go a long way, I thought, toward helping me with the art for the Earth's-Way campaign.

A couple of weeks after moving into the house I decided that I needed some good, sturdy, waterproof hiking boots, so I went into Cohocton to buy some. I'd been in the town before, of course, several times, but always with that sense of happy confusion that I get from being in a strange, new place and hoping I can find my way out, back to where I've come from, without having to stop and ask one of the locals for directions. This time I fully intended on talking to the locals—because this time I was on a tour of discovery.

I stopped first at a place called Czech's Garage, at the southern end of Cohocton, on its main street. (There are no more than a dozen streets in the town, and probably ten of those have been named after trees—Maple Street, Elm Street, Birch Drive, Willow Lane, and so on. Czech's Garage, I found, was owned and operated by a slow-talking man of forty or forty-five named Jerry Czech. I decided at once that he was probably typical of most of the men in the area. He was a little overweight, though not sloppy, wore a cap that had the name of a tractor company imprinted on it—as Jim Sandy had—bib overalls, a red flannel shirt, ankle-high blue sneakers, and several days' growth of white-patched beard, though he apparently had no white in his close-cropped dark hair.

I pulled my Toyota Corolla up to his unleaded pump, got out, saw him come out the door of his station toward me, waving me away from the pump.

"Sorry," I said, and stepped back.

He smiled thinly, and quickly. "Ain't got no self-serve in Cohocton; never had, never will." He took the nozzle from the pump, went around to the back of the car. It looked like he was having trouble finding the gas tank, so I said, pointing, "It's under the license plate."

He waved at me again, with agitation this time. "I know where it is; I been pumping gas a long time, so I know where it is." He flipped up the license plate, stuck the nozzle in, looked questioningly at me. "Fill 'er up for ya?"

I nodded. "Yes. Thanks."

He nodded.

I smiled at him, stepped forward, stuck my hand out. "My name's Jack Harris; I just moved into the Tanner house on Hunt's Hollow Road. I guess I'll be buying most of my gas here."

He shifted the nozzle from his right hand to his

left, shook my hand briefly, said, "Uh-huh, good to meetcha," let go of my hand, locked the nozzle on, went around to the front of the car. "Wanta open the hood there?"

"The oil's okay," I said.

"You sure?"

"Yes. Thanks."

He nodded. "You know you got crazy people living across the road? What'd you say your name was?"

"Jack Harris."

"Uh-huh. D'ja know that—about the crazy people?"

I shook my head, smiled as if he were trying to tell me a joke. "No, I didn't know that."

The gas stopped pumping; he went back, took the nozzle out, checked the pump. "Eleven-forty-three. That cash or charge?"

"Cash. What about these crazy people?" I was still smiling.

"And you got rattlesnakes up there, too. You said you was up on Hunt's Hollow?"

"Yes, that's right."

"You got rattlesnakes, then. On the hills especially, and in the rocks." I thought I saw a smile flit across his lips.

I said, "Bears, too?"

He nodded. "Yep. We had a bear up there once. It mauled a goat and a ten-year-old fat boy named Freddie Wilcox. Came down from Canada, I guess. I shot it. Me and a friend. Got it stuffed and in the laundry room." He went around to the front of the car, got a bottle of Windex from the top of one of the pumps, pulled a soiled rag from the back pocket of his overalls. "Get your windshield, Mr. Harris?"

"No. Thanks."

"Part of the service; might as well take it."

"No. I cleaned it at home."

"Didja?" Another quick smile appeared on his lips. He put the Windex back, held his hand out. "Eleven-forty-three."

I gave it to him, got in the car, said thanks again, and drove into Cohocton.

A quick tour of the main street confirmed that there was only one clothing store in town, a place called Buckles, Boots, & Buttons, which, considering the character of the town, I thought, wasn't quite right. I parked in front, went in, was greeted almost immediately by a short, thin, fiftyish woman wearing a long blue dress and horn-rimmed glasses.

"What can I do for you?" she asked pleasantly.

"Hi. I'm looking for some hiking boots."

"For hiking?"

"Yes."

"Or for climbing?" She'd been standing in front of a counter filled with men's dress pants. She stepped forward, gestured down a narrow aisle to her right that led to the rear of the store. I looked, saw a small display of men's leather boots in a far corner.

"For both, I guess," I said.

"Then you want a pair of hiking boots and a pair of climbing boots."

"Can't one be good for the other?"

She shook her head earnestly. "No, sir. Your
basic hiking boot has got to be lightweight, while
your basic climbing boot has got to be tough and
thick-soled. We got both—you buy both and you'll
be okay."

"I'll buy the hiking boot, then."

She was still holding her hand out. "Suit yourself,"
she said, and started down the aisle first, her gait
quick and stiff. She glanced back as I followed her.
"You buy a place in town?"

I smiled. "How'd you know I lived here?"

"You wouldn't be shopping here if you didn't."

I told her that was pretty logical. I told her about
the house I'd bought, started to say I thought Erika
and I would be happy in it, and she cut in, "It's
haunted, you know."

"What's haunted?" We were standing next to the
men's boot display now. It was only one step away
from being dismal.

"Your house. The Tanner house. It's haunted."

"By what?"

"By spooks."

She said it with a kind of casual intensity, as if she
were talking about a hole that people regularly fell
into. "You're serious?" I said.

And she said, "Not that I believe in spooks, of
course. They're probably geysers or something."

"Geysers?"

She nodded. "Boiling water shooting up outa the
ground. Geysers. Like Old Faithful. They shoot up

outa the ground and they look like spooks, especially at night.''

''You're joking with me, aren't you?''

She smiled very broadly, much too broadly, in fact, for my question. ''I don't joke much, but I do joke some,'' she said.

''And you're joking now?''

''I'm telling you what I've heard. Maybe I'm passing on a joke; maybe I'm not. Here's the hiking boots; I got your basic ankle-high, your mid-calf, and your knee-high. Which one would you like?''

I bought the mid-calf, which she approved of. ''Rattlesnakes can't get you, then,'' she said.

I smiled, said, ''Sure, thanks, and neither can the bears,'' and went to C. R. Boring Hardware to ask about gutters.

It was one of five hardware stores in Cohocton; they ran from slick to grim. C. R. Boring Hardware was somewhere in the middle. It was in a one-story red brick building that looked like it had been built within the past twenty years. That unlikely name (it still makes me smile) was painted in neat black block letters across the entire front of the store, above two large windows. The left-hand window had a display of gasoline cans in it—bright red five-gallon cans with spouts—and in the right window there were several dozen boxes of nails, screws, latches, and hooks. A crudely lettered sign hung on the window itself: END OF MONTH SALE: SERVE YOURSELF. It made me think of Jerry Czech and his animosity toward self-serve gas stations.

C. R. Boring was a very tall and perilously thin man, who was apparently well into his sixties; he was dressed in an ill-fitting gray suit. He'd pulled his white tie into a tight knot at his neck, so his grayish skin was pinched and folded there, and when I came in he looked up from behind the counter, at the back of the store, said " 'Scuse me, Frank" to a man standing in front of the counter, and called to me, "Be with you in a moment, sir."

"Gutters?" I said, and looked around questioningly.

"In a moment, sir," he said again, in the same stiffly polite tone.

"Sure," I said.

"In a way," I told Erika later that evening, as we sat and watched the fifth network rerun of *Children of the Corn*, which bored me but seemed to absorb Erika, "I guess I was disappointed."

She glanced quickly at me, then back at the TV. "Oh?" she said, clearly not interested. "How?"

I shrugged. "I think I wanted something more . . . rustic, more bucolic—"

"Bucolic?"

"Countryish, pastoral—"

"And it wasn't?"

"No. It was kind of phony. I know that sounds harsh. And I guess I don't mean *phony* phony: I don't think they're trying to trick anybody; I guess they're just being . . . people—"

Again she glanced at me; she smiled bemusedly, said, "Of course they're just being people, Jack.

What'd you expect them to be—porcupines?'' She cocked her head to one side, added, ''Huh?'' then looked at the TV again and muttered, ''I don't understand this,'' low enough that I realized she was talking to herself.

I said, ''Sure. It would have been a lot easier to deal with porcupines,'' paused briefly, then continued on another subject, ''What do you think of this, Erika?'' I cleared my throat in prelude, held my hand up as if making a solemn pronouncement. She looked at me. ''From Nature's Table to Yours—Earth's— Way 100% natural and wholesome vitamin and mineral supplements.''

''It's cluttered,'' she said.

''What's cluttered about it?'' My feelings were hurt. ''It won't look cluttered in print.''

''The last part. It's cluttered; it's unnecessary.''

''The client wants it there. Besides, it really is necessary; it's important.'' I realized that I was whining.

Erika shrugged. ''It's your client, your work, Jack. You asked my opinion; I gave it to you.''

I shrugged. ''How about 'From Nature's Table to Your Table'? That's pretty good, don't you think?''

''It's simpler, yes.''

''Or maybe 'Out of the earth and into your kitchen.' '' I paused, thought about that one, realized that I liked it quite a lot. I repeated it slowly, with feeling, '' 'Out of the *earth* . . . and *into* your kitchen.' Christ, that's great; that's really great! Don't you think that's great, Erika?''

She said nothing.

I repeated, " 'Out of the earth and into your kitchen.' Don't you think that's great? I mean, don't you think that *means* something?!"

"I'd rather not discuss it now, Jack. I'm watching this . . . movie." She nodded briskly at the TV.

"Oh? Why don't you want to discuss it? *I* want to discuss it."

"I'd just rather not, Jack. I've got problems of my own—"

"You mean the store?"

"Sure. I mean the store. It gets me down."

"Are you selling any records?"

She nodded vaguely. "Of course I am." She stood. "I'm going to go do some reading, Jack. Okay? This movie makes me nervous; you make me nervous." She stopped, closed her eyes, shook her head, went on, "I guess I'm just plain nervous."

"Sure," I said. "I understand," though I didn't, and she turned and left.

CHAPTER FOUR

She came up from doing the laundry in the cellar the following evening and said, "Jack? The house is haunted!" The look on her face was an odd mixture of bemusement, frustration, and anger—as if she wanted to throw her hands into the air and say, *Now, what are we going to do?* "The house is haunted. And I don't like it."

I said the predictable: "Erika, I've known you how long now—six, seven years?—and I had no idea you believed in ghosts."

She cocked her head in confusion. "I thought everyone believed in ghosts. Don't you?"

I shrugged. "I suppose I do."

She looked annoyed. I added, my tone more serious, "Yes. I do. I believe in ghosts, Erika." I didn't stop to consider whether I was telling the truth or not. I didn't think I was. I was, at that point, trying to avoid a confrontation.

Erika said, "But you don't believe that *this* house is haunted, right?"

Again, I said the predictable: "Tell me why you think it's haunted and I can give you a rational answer."

"Because," she started, her tone suddenly stiff; she pointed at the floor to indicate the cellar—"there are people *talking* down there."

I nodded at the TV, which was on, volume low: "No. It was just the TV, Erika. I've heard the same sort of thing before. It sounds like there are people living in the walls, doesn't it?" I paused; she said nothing. I went on, "But there aren't any people in the walls. If there were, they wouldn't be talking, would they?"

"No," she said, coolly.

"You think my theory's full of holes, don't you?"

"Yes," she said, still coolly. She nodded at the TV. "I can hardly hear that, and I'm in the same room with it, Jack. How in the hell am I going to hear it down in the cellar?"

I shrugged again. "Weird acoustics, I don't know."

She said nothing.

"Okay, then—tell me what these spooks were talking about, Erika?"

"There was only one."

"Oh?"

"Yes. And I'm not sure what he was talking about. Something about the dark."

"Oh? You didn't hear every word, Erika?"

"No. Not every word. He mumbles."

"Oh. He mumbles."

"Stop that, damnit!"

"Stop humoring you?"

"Yes. The house is haunted, and when you care to talk about it further, I'll be in my music room." And she turned and left.

I was curious, of course. I went into the cellar, said a few stupid things—"Hey, Mr. Spook, where are you? Come out, Mr. Spook"—then went to Erika's music room and told her I'd found nothing at all in the cellar.

"Of course you didn't," she told me. "How are you going to find a ghost unless it wants to be found?"

It was a good question. I had no answer for it, so the subject was dropped.

A week later, Erika said to me over dinner, "I passed a place called Granada today, Jack."

"Oh?" I said.

She nodded, stuck a forkful of my homemade fettuccine Alfredo into her mouth, looked appreciative. "I took a different route home. You drive the same damned route every day, and it gets pretty boring." She pointed with her fork at her plate of fettuccine

Alfredo. "This is good stuff, Jack. Really." She tossed her head so her dark hair fell in back of her shoulders.

"Thanks," I said.

"There were POSTED signs everywhere, but the place was deserted, so I drove through." She shook her head, scowled. "God, it was awfully grim. Remember Love Canal, near Buffalo, Jack?"

"Yes," I said. "Entire little community all deserted and boarded up, right? Didn't it have something to do with a chemical dump?"

She nodded. "This was the same kind of thing, I think. Several of the houses—and these were *nice* houses, Jack; I mean, these were $150,000 houses, at least—several of these houses had burned, but most of them looked like they'd simply been abandoned."

"And no one was there, Erika?"

She shook her head. "Not a soul. Lots of wildlife. I saw six or seven deer, a whole mess of squirrels, and bluejays, and I think I saw a raccoon, too. But no people." She popped another forkful of fettuccine into her mouth and chewed very deliberately.

"Sounds . . . intriguing," I said.

"It was, Jack. It really was. I mean—it was spooky, sure—"

"Spooky?" I cut in, and nodded to my left to indicate the area where Jim Sandy had made his discovery. "Like *that* was spooky?"

"No, Jack. *Good* spooky. Like going to a horror movie. It's at a distance, so it's not real. I could drive away from it. It's *there*"—she pointed quickly to her left, to the east—"I *know* it's there. But it's not *here*, is it?" She pointed stiffly at the kitchen floor.

I grinned.

"Is it?" she repeated.

"I don't know," I said. "How do you know it didn't follow you home?"

"Shithead!"

"Just trying to scare the pants off you, that's all."

She grinned a big, playful, inviting grin. "Maybe you did," she said.

"Oh?" I said. "Can I find out?"

"Sure," she answered. "Any time."

"How about now?"

"Yes," she said.

So I did, and I had.

"Sort of like what you imagine people wore to royal costume parties, huh?" she said at breakfast several mornings later.

"What are you talking about, Erika?"

"I'm talking about that 'part of a nose and forehead' you said were found here."

"Oh." We were seated at the kitchen table, a glass top on a steel pedestal that we'd bought at a restaurant supply house several years before. There was a saucer with a couple of pieces of whole wheat toast on the table, a coffeepot, a pitcher of orange juice. I lifted the coffeepot. "More?"

Erika nodded. I said as I poured, "That's pretty grim. You surprise me."

"It was a joke," she said.

I smiled, set the coffeepot down. "We won't do too much digging around here, okay?"

"I was thinking of starting a garden, Jack." She took a quick sip of her coffee. "In that little flat open area near the privet hedge, in the spring. And if I find anything . . . tacky, I'll mark it with some string and save it for you."

"Save it for me? What am I going to do with it?" This was a tense sort of humor we were sharing. "Start a collection?"

She broke a piece of toast in half, studied it a moment, took a tiny bite of it. "Sure," she said. She took a larger bite. "You can start a collection, Jack. A body parts collection. And one day you can put a whole man together." She stuffed what remained of the toast into her mouth and said something unintelligible.

"Huh?" I said.

She swallowed, grinned. "We'll call you Doctor Frankenstein." She pronounced *Frankenstein* "Fronk-en-steen," the way Gene Wilder did. "Jack Fronk-en-steen and his whole man from the earth." Another grin, broader and stiffer. She shrugged. "Or maybe it's a woman, Jack. Did you ever think of that?"

"No," I said.

"I mean, an arm that looks like a rolled-up grocery bag doesn't necessarily have to be a man's arm. It could be a woman's; it could be a man's; it could be a child's."

"Maybe," I said, and grinned.

"What are you grinning about, Jack?"

My grin broadened. I said in deep, sepulchral tones, "Out of the *earth* and into your *bedroom*, ha, ha, ha!"

She said, eyes closed, and a little shiver running over her, "Let's drop it, okay?"

"Sorry?" I said.

"I said"—her huge brown eyes popped open and she stared hard at me—"let's drop it. That's not funny!"

"Sorry," I said again, though in apology this time.

Twenty years ago, in the park through which I walked home from school five nights a week, I called to Harry Simms, "Harry, it's me, it's Jack Harris. Come on out, Harry, what are you tryin' to prove, anyway?" I'd thought of running away a number of times, though mostly just for the hell of it, and I'd thought that the park would make a good starting point. So, if Harry had run away, as everyone thought he had, he might still be there. And besides, I'd seen him; I'd heard him scream, "I can't breathe, I can't breathe!" as he swept past me, which I thought was a kind of a joke because it was the same thing he'd said earlier in the day, when he'd taken it hard in the gut during battle ball. He'd gone to his knees, hands pressed into his stomach, mouth wide, and he'd whispered, "I can't breathe, I can't breathe!" It scared the hell out of everyone, of course, but it turned out that he was only being melodramatic, that he really could breathe but that for some damned reason, he'd *forgotten* how.

"Harry, goddamnit!" I called in the park three days after seeing him there. He wasn't what I'd have called a good close friend, but he'd been to my house a couple of times, and I'd been to his, and I figured that if *he* thought he had a good, close friend at school, it was me.

That evening in the park it was sharply colder than it had been three nights earlier, although the air was dead still. I called to Harry Simms a number of times, and, of course, I got no answer. I heard only a high whining noise like the noise mosquitoes make. And that's what I thought it was, in fact, although the night was far too cold for mosquitoes.

I didn't realize until just a few months ago that what I was hearing was my sometime-friend Harry Simms weeping as he melted slowly and purposefully into the earth.

I think a lot of people had friends like Harry.

CHAPTER FIVE

It was a while before we were able to take a walking tour of our property. Erika was spending long hours at her record store and I had my own work to do as well as lots of fix-up jobs around the house.

Also, it rained too much. It rained every day for two weeks after Jim Sandy gave up on his trench digging—a soft, gray, constant drizzle that became a part of the background noise and ambiance of the house. God, it was depressing. When we were home together and that dismal rain was coming down, we moved about as if in slow motion, as if the air itself were thickening and we had to work very hard to walk in it. We played cards; we listened to music—Erika liked Rachmaninoff, the Beatles, Leonard Cohen—we made love three or four times a week (less than usual, but still noteworthy considering the depressing weather and our overwork) and took turns cooking. My specialties had everything to do with pasta. I'm a whiz at making pasta dishes. Pasta is heavy, hearty food, and I like the feeling of fullness it gives me. Erika's tastes are more eclectic, and artistic. She likes bean sprouts, falafel, goose liver paté (and, of course, my homemade fettuccine Alfredo), and she treats the preparation of food with great respect and love. She said once, "We have only what the soil gives us," and then grinned, as if embarrassed, because it was the kind of deeply philosophical remark which, from me, would have embarrassed her.

But the rain stopped sometime early in January. The soil dried enough that we could walk on it without sinking to mid-calf, and we set off, up our mountain, with our wiry black tomcat, Orphan, following and talking to us constantly—a quick, high-pitched meow that sounded just like the word "now."

I was thankful for the hiking boots I'd bought, because I'd grown to believe most of the stories the locals had told me, especially the stories about rattlesnakes.

I'd been told many other things about life in the area—that there were bobcats and foxes, that the raccoons would tear our garbage up if we didn't hide it, that there were packs of feral dogs roaming about, and, of course, that crazy people lived high up on the mountain across the road from us. I'd come to the conclusion that it was best to believe most of what I heard. After a while I found that some of it was false and some of it was true, but by then it didn't make any difference.

Erika and I walked north first, down a wide, grassy path that skirted the foot of our mountain for three-quarters of a mile. This path had once been a county road and had been unofficially named Goat's Head Road by the people in Cohocton, though no one could say exactly why. On the survey map of our property, it's simply called *Old County Road Number 12/Abandoned*. It continues well beyond our northern boundary, but when we got to the place where the surveyor had put up his wooden boundary markers, we turned east and started to climb our mountain.

Erika said then, "Remember, Jack, if we find anything, it's yours."

And I said, playing the ignorant, "I don't understand."

"Body parts, Jack. If we find any hands or feet or legs or . . . or anything else, then you've got to deal with it. Okay?"

"We won't find any body parts," I said.

"Is that a promise?"

I nodded earnestly. "You have my solemn promise, Erika. I have searched every available inch of our estate with my new, soon-to-be-patented Body Parts Detector, and I can assure you—"

"Can it, Jack."

I canned it.

She was dressed very warmly in a blue ski jacket, a brown turtleneck sweater, jeans, her hiking boots, and brown leather gloves. I would have been sweating in an outfit like that—the temperature was well into the forties, and the air was damp from the recent rains. But Erika was always easily chilled. Most evenings that winter she spent an hour or so seated on the floor in front of the living room fireplace, her bare feet up close to the grating and a look of deep comfort and satisfaction on her face.

"How long's this been going on, Jack?" she asked after a while. We were about a hundred feet up the mountain then, and trying hard to find an area where we wouldn't slide two feet down for every foot of progress up.

"You mean the body parts thing, Erika?" I'd found some solid ground. She was trying, with much difficulty, to pull herself further up the mountain from it by clinging to the thin branch of a dead oak tree. I planted both my hands firmly on her rear end and pushed. It took her by surprise. Her upper body lurched backward; her arms went wide, and with a small, high-pitched squeak of surprise, she began to fall. I caught her, held her a moment with my arms around her chest, and noticed that her breathing had become quick and shallow, as if she were in shock.

I whispered to her, trying to sound playful, "Sorry

about that, kiddo,'' but she made no response, so I continued, ''Really. I'm sorry,'' and she shrugged out of my loose grip, turned halfway, and shook her head quickly.

''No,'' she said; I heard tension in her voice. ''No, it's all right. It's just that for a moment I felt like I was being . . . swallowed up.''

''Swallowed up. By what?''

She made a visible effort to bring her breathing back to normal. ''I don't know, Jack. By this mountain.'' She smiled sheepishly, embarrassed. ''By nothing.''

We saw a man at the top of our mountain when we were halfway up. We yelled ''Hello'' to him, and Erika added, ''Who are you?''—but he was a good distance from us, and we realized that he probably couldn't hear us. He was walking several feet back from the crest of the mountain, so we saw him only from the waist up, and I guessed that he was wearing jeans and a denim jacket, though from my vantage point it was hard to tell. Erika yelled to him again, ''Who are you?'' And added, ''This is private property, you know!'' I think he turned his head slightly when she said that.

I believe that he smiled.

''Yes,'' I yelled, ''private property!''

And he was gone.

Erika turned to me. ''That *is* our property up there, isn't it, Jack?''

''I think it is,'' I answered. ''I'll check the map.''

''Yes,'' she said. ''Do that.''

* * *

It is true, of course, that our memories sustain us. They give the present a backdrop, scenery, substance; they tell us who we are and what we're becoming. They sing to us and caress us. And sometimes they make us sit for hours, quietly, unmoving, and unchanging. As if that will put time off, and the moments will not happen. I used to do that even then, at the house.

I used to look at her and tell her how very beautiful she was. She liked that. She'd blush and say thank you, but that she wasn't, really, that it was all just an illusion. "You don't take compliments well," I'd tell her.

"Just telling you what's real," she'd say.

And I'd chuckle because I thought she was trying to be philosophical, cryptic, and humble. But I was wrong.

I went into Cohocton for some art supplies later that day to a shop called Ulla's Arts and Handicrafts. It was run by a pleasant, middle-aged Swedish woman and her husband, who was usually somewhere else when I visited. I'd been to the shop before, and when I walked in, Ulla looked up from behind the counter, said hello to me in Swedish, caught herself, said hello in English, thought a moment, and added, "Hello, Mr. Harris."

"Jack," I said.

"Hello, Jack." Her mouth had a constant, flat smile on it, not a vacuous kind of smile, but the kind that asked without words how she could help me. But it was also oddly defensive, as if she were trying to get the jump on bad news. "Are you settling in up there?"

"We're trying," I said.

"And have those people been to see you?"

"What people, Ulla?"

"The people who live across the road, Jack." Her smile flickered. "I don't know their names."

"No," I said. "No one's been to see us."

"They're crazy people, Jack." She put her forefinger to her temple. "They'll come and bother you. They bother everyone."

I said nothing for a long moment. This wasn't the first I'd heard of the crazy people who lived across the road, of course, and I wasn't sure that Ulla, like the others who'd talked with me about them, wasn't having fun with me. It had become clear that the locals took an almost perverse pleasure in trying to scare newcomers, especially if they were city people and therefore unfamiliar with country life.

"Are you joking with me?" I gave her a half smile that was designed to tell her that I wasn't totally without a sense of humor, that if she was joking it was okay.

"Joking?" She shook her head. "No. I'm not joking. There are people living on the mountain across the road from you, and they are crazy."

"How are they crazy, Ulla?"

She lowered her head in thought. After a moment she looked up and said, "I don't know. I've heard about them. My customers tell me about them. They tell me they're like the people in that movie *Deliverance*. But I don't know how, exactly. I can't tell you." She turned her head slightly to one side. "Now, what can I do for you, today?"

The following morning I answered a soft knock at the front door—I wouldn't have heard it if I'd been anywhere but in the living room or the library—to find a man in his early twenties, dressed in a sport coat, white shirt, gray pants. He gave me a big, open grin, as if *he* were welcoming *me* to the house.

"Hi," he began, and stuck his hand out. I took it. He pumped my hand a few times, not too long, let it go. "My name's Allan Sibbe. I represent Dominion Properties, of Colorado." He reached into his sport coat pocket, withdrew a business card, handed it to me. "My card," he went on. The card read: "Allan Sibbe: Sales Representative: Dominion Properties/ Colorado," and gave a phone number.

"I'm not interested in buying property," I told the young man. "Sorry."

"I'm not selling property," he said. "Keep the card, please." I stuffed it into my pants pocket. "I'm not empowered to sell property, Mr. Harris."

"How'd you know my name?"

"Your mailbox." He turned his head to the left and nodded backward to indicate it. "What I'm doing, Mr. Harris, is *showing* properties. I'm not going to deny that these properties are for sale. One does not show properties that *aren't* for sale, does one?"

"No," I conceded.

"Of course not. My point being that real estate—
land, Mr. Harris—is your very best investment. But of
course that investment must be made at the right
moment. Otherwise it's not an investment, is it? No.
It's a risk. And the business of Dominion Properties
is to eliminate risk, where possible—and it is often
possible, Mr. Harris, as you'll see—and where it is
not possible to refine it, to delineate it, to *limit* it to
its very *lowest* limits." Another grin. He was clearly
enjoying himself. "*Land* is your best investment. It
stays. It lasts. It *is*! It produces. It nurtures. It be-
comes what you want it to become." A brief pause.
"Do you understand that, Mr. Harris?"

"Sure," I said, though it wasn't entirely true.

"Of course you do. Everyone does." Then he
added in a whisper, as if it were a secret, "They just
won't admit it, will they?" Then he went on, voice
at a normal level, "No sir, you can't make a better
investment than land. This is the good earth here;
we're talking about the soil, the thing that feeds us
and keeps us alive." He was starting to sound a bit
fanatical, and I wanted to bring the encounter to a
close.

"Thank you," I said. "Thank you very much—"

"Perhaps, if I could come inside . . ."

"No, I don't think so. You'll have to excuse me; I
have things to do."

"I'm sorry, too."

"Good-bye," I said politely but firmly, and I
closed the door. I heard him shuffle across the porch,
pull the screen door open, close it behind him, and
leave.

CHAPTER SIX

My mother has never taken to Erika. She makes no bones about it, although she's usually a very tactful woman.

"It's as if I need to know more about her," she said once, shortly after Erika and I were married.

I said, "What more do you need to know?" I was ready to give her a list of all that she did know about Erika—her age, her education, her tastes in food and art, her political and religious views, et cetera.

She cut in, "That's not enough, Jack."

"It would be with anyone else, Mom."

"Maybe. Maybe not. But with her, with Erika, it's as if those things are merely . . . accoutrements."

I chuckled.

"I mean it, Jack." My mother can sound pretty severe when she wants to. I stopped chuckling.

"I don't know what that means—'accoutrements.' "

"It means things added on, Jack. It means—"

"I know what the word means. I just don't know how it applies to Erika."

She thought a moment. "I mean it's all surface; it's like it's been tacked on."

"You're saying she's a phony? Is that what you're saying, Mom? Because I don't see her that way. I don't see her that way at all."

She shook her head, held her hand up. "No, Jack. No. Not in the least. She's not a phony; I think she's very genuine. I just think that I would like to know more, as I said before, but—I don't think I ever will. I don't think I ever *can*."

I should have gotten upset with her. After all, she wasn't giving Erika a fair chance. But I said nothing. And that's where the conversation ended.

My mother visited shortly after we moved into the house. She brought us a bottle of Dom Perignon, which all of us shared—including my brother Will, who had come up with my mother. I proposed a toast: "To us," I said, "to the house," and my mother and Will joined in. My mother was trying very hard to be friendly to Erika that day. They went for a short walk together, down Goat's Head Road, and Erika pointed out the cabin there. They discussed Erika's plans to start a garden, and together they scouted out the best area for it. Things looked pretty damned promising between them, and I thought that at last my mother had grown to like Erika. Later, however, when she and I were alone—Erika and Will had gone into Cohocton to shop for dinner—she said, "I'm sorry, Jack; I'm sorry, but I still don't like her." She stopped abruptly, then hurried on, "No, that's not true. No. I like her. I like the . . . person she is. I just have a mother's distrust of her." She grinned at the phrase. "That sounds awfully old-fashioned, doesn't it? And judgmental."

"Yes," I said, which surprised her.

She grinned again. "It's not judgmental, Jack. At least I don't intend it to be judgmental." A pause. After several moments she continued, "Your brother is quite fond of her. I'm sure you've noticed."

I took a deep breath to show that the fact that Will liked Erika meant very little to me. "Yes, Mom. I've noticed."

"Of course you have. And why shouldn't he be fond of her? My God, Jack—Erika's a knockout."

I shook my head. "She's not a knockout, Mom. She's good-looking, sure—"

"I'm not talking about her appearance, Jack. I'm talking about her *aura*."

Now it was my turn to grin. "Her aura, Mom?"

"Yes." She had a look of deadly seriousness about her. "The way she appears to men."

"How would you know about that, Mom?" Another grin. It was a frivolous question, and I wanted her to know that I realized it.

"Women know things about other women. And I know this about Erika: Men find her very, very appealing."

"And that's why you don't like her?" I didn't like the way the conversation was tending. "This is all getting kind of Freudian, Mom."

"Don't flatter yourself, Jack. When I say I have a mother's distrust of her, I'm not talking about being jealous. I'm talking about what she'll do to you without even knowing it."

"That's high melodrama, Mom."

"Life is high melodrama, Jack."

Which is when Will and Erika appeared in the kitchen doorway, grocery bags in hand. Will is ten years older than I, a good six inches taller, but twenty pounds lighter. He was about as "dressed down" as I'd seen him in years—black tailored slacks, a Harris tweed sports coat, a light blue button-down shirt. "Wonderoast Chicken," he announced.

"Whatever that is," said Erika, just behind him in the doorway, holding up another grocery bag. "And macaroni salad, beans, fruit salad, and . . . and . . ." She peeked into the bag, looked up squeamishly, fetchingly. "Something else. I have no idea what it is."

"We'll find out, I'm sure," I said.

*   *   *

Will said, over dinner, "Is there a migrant labor camp in the area, Jack?"

I nodded, took a small bite of Wonderoast Chicken, which was lean and tasty, said, "A few. But there aren't many migrant laborers. Especially this time of year."

Will shrugged. "I saw some people on the road—"

My mother cut in, "This is good chicken, Jack."

I nodded at Erika. "Erika and Will bought it, Mom."

Will said, "Maybe they were backpackers or something. You probably get a lot of that type up here, right, Jack?"

"That type, Will?"

"Sure. The backpacking type. Back-to-the-landers." He smiled smugly.

"Will," I said, "that's kind of what Erika and I are."

His smug smile broadened. "Sure you are, Jack. Sure you are. I'd say you're about as establishment as a ten-dollar bill."

To end the conversation there, I said, "Maybe you're right, Will," then asked my mother, "How are the Twigs, Mom?" The Twigs are a woman's group she's involved in.

"They're okay. A little stodgy," she added, and that's when the singing started. An aria from *Carmen*. It was coming from outside, to the south.

"Good God," Will said.

"What's that?" my mother said. "It sounds like *Carmen*."

Will said that it was *Carmen*. Erika, whose back was to the house's southern wall, glanced quickly toward it. "Yes," she said matter-of-factly, "it's from *Carmen*."

"Is there a house over that way, Jack?" Will asked.

"No," I answered.

Erika looked back at the table, munched some more of the chicken, "This is full of grease," she muttered.

I went to the kitchen door, opened it, and peered out into the early evening darkness. I saw nothing. I pushed the storm door open. The singing seemed to be coming from within the woods a hundred feet away. I felt someone behind me. It was Will.

"Nice voice," he said. "Some neighbor woman, you think?"

"Singing *Carmen* in the middle of my woods at 8:30 at night, Will? The people are strange around here, but I doubt they're that strange."

"Obviously, they are," Will said.

My mother appeared behind Will. "Is she a friend of yours, Jack? A neighbor?"

"Will and I were just discussing that, Mom."

"I don't know what you were discussing, Jack," she said testily.

The singing stopped.

"Someone's record player," Will said. "Sound probably carries awfully well in these hills, Jack."

"Probably."

"It was nice while it lasted, anyway," my mother said.

And from behind us, Erika called, "Come back and eat. It's getting cold. No one likes cold meat."

Our first lovemaking was an event.

It happened at night, in January, at the end of a cul-de-sac where new houses that had gone up several months earlier still waited for buyers. A single streetlamp cast a frigid blue glow on us, and even today, seven years later, I can get an amazing mental picture of the two of us writhing naked in the snow, much too involved in what we were doing to care about frostbite.

She caught me by surprise. I was taking her back to her apartment after dinner and a movie and my mind was furiously at work thinking of ways to get her into bed. My mind had been furiously at work on that particular problem, in fact, for the two weeks and a few days that I'd known her. That was part of the game, wasn't it? A part of the conquest? Sure it was a holdover from senior high school, but it was a holdover that I enjoyed.

She looked earnestly at me from the passenger seat and she said, "Jack?—Let's fuck."

It threw me. "Let's fuck?" I said. I grinned nervously, glanced at her, looked back at the road.

"Don't you want to fuck?" she asked. That threw me, too, because her tone was much the same kind of tone that she'd use to ask if I wanted to have another cup of coffee. "Don't you want to fuck?" she repeated; *Don't you want another cup of coffee?*

I answered, feeling foolish and ill-at-ease, "You mean, just like that?"

She was wearing a beige skirt, a blue blouse, a long, bulky, white coat. She shrugged out of the coat, tossed it into the back seat, started unbuttoning the blouse.

"Erika," I said, "I'm driving."

She chuckled quickly, continued unbuttoning the blouse. "So, you'll stop driving and we'll fuck."

"Just like that?" I said again. She had her blouse unbuttoned completely; she hesitated; I glanced at her, saw in the light of streetlamps that goosebumps were rising on her breasts. I looked back at the road: "Jesus, Erika!" I was smiling; I couldn't help it. "Jesus, you'll make me have an accident."

"No"—she reached across the seat, put her hand on my crotch—"don't have an accident, Jack." She nodded to indicate a street sign just ahead. "Pull in there. We'll fuck in there." Underneath the street sign there was a sign that read, "Knollwood Acres: Prestige Living." I pulled into Knollwood Acres, stopped at the end of the cul-de-sac. By then, Erika was naked, and when I touched her I could feel the goosebumps on her.

"You'll catch a cold," I breathed. We were still in the car.

"Shut up," she said sharply.

I straightened in the seat, put my hands on the

steering wheel; "You're confusing the hell out of me, Erika."

"I want to fuck. I need to fuck. Everyone needs to fuck." She got out of the car, stood with her back to me and the bluish glow of the streetlamp on her; she stiffened, clenched her fists at her sides and screamed into the still, cold air, "Fuck me, Jack! Everyone needs to fuck!"

What could I do? There were no lights on in the big houses all around us so I got out of the car, went to her, and put my arms around her; I was pretending, even to myself, that I was attempting to warm her with my body. But that pretense faded fast, and moments later, I had my pants off, then my shirt, and we were in six inches of snow making love.

I used to mention that night every now and then because it really was an amazing night and I thought it showed, beautifully, what really primitive creatures we were beneath it all. But, slowly, she grew to resent it, and once even grew angry when I brought it up—"That's not the way *civilized* human beings behave!" were her words.

"I'm sorry," I said, and meant it.

She shook her head slowly, in self-condemnation. "So am I, Jack. It's just something kind of personal. You understand, I'm sure."

"Uh—huh," I said, "I understand," though I didn't. The subject hasn't been mentioned since.

CHAPTER SEVEN

Several nights after my mother and Will visited I was awakened shortly after midnight by the frantic roar of snowmobile engines. I nudged Erika, asleep beside me.

"Erika? Wake up."

She grumbled "No," turned over, and murmured, "Go back to sleep, Jack."

I got out of bed and went to the window that overlooked the road and the mountain on the other side of it. The drapes were closed; I drew them aside a few inches.

I would have guessed, from the noise level, that

the snowmobiles were in our front yard. They weren't. They were across the road, on the mountain, ten or twelve of them, all in a line, the white glare of their headlights bobbing on a narrow path that wound up the mountain.

I watched for several minutes. Now and again, one of the snowmobiles would stop, as if it were having trouble, and the others would stop too. There'd be loud talking, some curses—the snowmobiles were at a distance of at least half a mile, but sound carried well on the still night air—and at last the line would get going again. They were on their way to what looked like a good-sized house halfway up the mountain. I could see the suggestion of lighted windows through the trees, the underside of a roof.

After a few minutes, Erika said behind me, "What's going on, Jack? What's all that noise?"

I said, without turning to look at her, "Just a bunch of snowmobilers, Erika."

"Oh," she said, as if that were all the explanation she needed and she could go back to sleep.

"I think those are the crazy people they told me about," I went on.

Erika said nothing.

"A bunch of crazy snowmobilers." People who get their kicks out of making lots of noise in the middle of the night are essentially easy to deal with, I decided; you either put up with their noise or you do something about it.

"If this keeps up," I went on, more to myself than to Erika, "I'll have words with them."

"Sure, Jack," she whispered.

The following morning, a Monday, I went across the road. I found the snowmobiles' tracks in the mud and snow, though little else. I thought about going to the house and giving whoever happened to be there my two-cents' worth about the roar of snowmobile engines at 12:30 in the morning, but my cowardice got in the way. I told myself, instead, that if it happened again, *then* I'd talk to someone—and started back.

I heard a man call from behind me, "Wait there, please," and looked around. He was on the path that led to the house. He was tall, dark-haired; he wore brown pants, a red flannel shirt, and an orange hunting vest. He was also carrying a rifle, barrel down, in his right hand, and he was walking very quickly toward me. He raised his left hand a little when he was still a good fifty feet away and said again, "Wait there, please."

"Sure," I said.

He stopped several feet from me and smiled thinly. "Tell me who you are, please," he said. He had a broad, flat face, a wide nose, and small brown eyes—it was actually the face of a fat man, and it looked ludicrous on his tall, thin body.

"Who are you?" I said.

He nodded to indicate the house at the middle of the mountain. "I live there. My name's Martin. And this"—he nodded toward his feet to indicate the path we were on—"is private property."

I shrugged. "Then I'll leave," I said.

"It's not that I'm trying to be unfriendly," he said, and his thin smile reappeared, "but we really do like our privacy, Mr. Harris."

"How'd you know my name?"

He pointed at my mailbox across the road. "Easy enough," he said.

"Oh." I paused, added, "Who's 'we'?"

" 'We'?"

"You said, 'We like our privacy.' Who's 'we'?"

He nodded a couple of times, as if to indicate that he understood. "Yes. That's me and my family, Mr. Harris. There are quite a few of us—"

"I know. I heard you last night."

His thin smile broadened. "Did we disturb you? I'm sorry." He sounded sincere. "I'll try to see that it doesn't happen again."

"Thanks. I don't mean to complain, it's just that my wife—"

"Of course you don't mean to complain, Mr. Harris. And I don't mean to sound unfriendly, either." He paused, smiled very broadly, then said, "But our privacy really is very important to us."

"As is mine."

"Of course. But for different reasons, I'm sure." It was clearly a spontaneous remark. And from his quick and short-lived frown, I got the idea that he regretted it at once. He nodded toward my house, smiled a dismissal. "Good day, Mr. Harris."

I said nothing; I turned and walked back to the house.

*   *   *

We had trouble with moles early in March. Spring seemed to have arrived early; we had little snow, and what snow there was melted quickly in temperatures that were in the forties and fifties. So the moles appeared, and our cats had a field day with them. They killed them, skinned them, and left the bloody carcasses in spots inside the house where we'd be sure to find them and, I assume, see what wonderful hunters they were. The moles were of varying sizes. Some were as small as a man's thumb, others much larger, and they apparently numbered in the hundreds around the house.

The killing of the moles had a strange effect on Erika. At first she didn't seem to care much, beyond the fact that neither of us enjoyed finding tiny corpses in the house every morning (our cats came and went through a small pet door I'd installed in the laundry room). But after a week or so I found her weeping over one.

"It's only a mole, Erika," I said.

"Of course it's only a mole," she said, and it was clear from her tone that she wanted the subject dropped.

Several mornings later I found her weeping over another one; the cats had left it at the bottom of the stairway.

"Erika," I said, "you're beginning to worry me."

"I don't mean to," she said, swiped at her tears with the back of her hand, and sniffled, "I'm sorry."

I got several paper towels, and scooped up what remained of the mole. "I'll go and toss it into the woods, Erika.'' It was what I'd been doing with the other animals the cats had killed.

She shook her head. "No. I want you to bury it, Jack.''

I grinned. I couldn't help it. "I'd rather not.''

"It came from the earth, Jack.'' She hesitated, turned back one of the folds of paper towel to reveal the tiny red body within, stared at it a moment, then looked earnestly at me. "So put it back *into* the earth.''

I grinned again, nervously this time, because I could hear a strange kind of tension in her voice. "Sure, Erika,'' I said. "If that's what you'd like.'' And I buried the mole in our backyard, close to where what we liberally referred to as "our lawn'' blended with the weeds and thickets that were the beginning of the woods.

Several days later I set out on a solo trip into Cohocton for dessert fixings. Erika wanted sundaes; she liked hot fudge on Häagen-Dazs vanilla, with chopped nuts and real whipped cream; I liked everything but the chopped nuts. On the way I happened upon the jogger I'd seen earlier in the year. He was sitting on the edge of the road—his head down, his knees up, as if he'd gotten dizzy and was trying to correct it—in front of an open field that had a weathered FOR SALE sign in it, several acres of vineyards to the north, a trailer that looked abandoned to the south. I stopped next to him and rolled the passenger window down. "Hi. You okay?''

His hair was dark, straight and nearly to his shoulders, his skin almost as dark, as if from a very good tan, and his body, in blue running shorts and a sleeveless white T-shirt, was well-muscled and lean. He shook his head a little, though he didn't look up.

"You're not okay?" I thought he had misunderstood my question.

He whispered hoarsely, "I'll be okay. Thanks."

I didn't believe him. He sounded awful, as if on the verge of passing out. "Are you cold?" The temperature was hovering, I guessed, at around fifty.

He nodded, though he still didn't look up. "Yes. I am now. Not when I run. I'm not cold when I run."

I put the car's flashers on, and went to the jogger, got down on my haunches, held my hand out. "My name's Jack Harris."

He looked up briefly, glanced at my hand, looked down again. "Hi, Mr. Harris. Thanks, but I'll be okay." His face was spectacularly average. It could have jumped off a *Popular Mechanics* ad for power saws. The eyes were brown, like Erika's, but not so large and appealing; the nose was straight, the mouth full, the cheeks a little hollow. There were probably ten million faces like it; if you took the crowd of male faces at a football game or a boxing match or a topless bar and mixed them together and made one face out of them, you'd get this jogger's face.

I said, "Sure, you'll be okay. But maybe I can give you a lift somewhere."

He shook his head. A little chuckle came from him.

"Did I say something funny?" I asked.

He said, his voice a bit steadier now, "Did you ever have a dream that you were running . . ." He paused, cleared his throat, went on, "Where you were running from . . . something. Anything. It doesn't matter what. You were running. And after a while, after a short while, you realized that you weren't getting far?" Another pause; he looked quizzically up at me.

I said, "Sure. Everyone's had a dream like that."

He nodded, lowered his head again. "And the reason you weren't getting far, Mr. Harris, was that your feet were glued to the earth?"

I nodded. "Yes," I said, "but not since I was a kid." I realized that it sounded like a kind of value judgment, so I said again, "Everyone's had that kind of dream, I think, at one time or another."

"I have it all the time."

"Uh-huh," I said for lack of anything better to say. I get embarrassed, a little tongue-tied when strangers begin opening up their private lives to me. It happens a lot. It happened with Erika, in fact, when we first met. I added, "I'm sorry, it must be . . . difficult."

He nodded, his head still lowered. "It is. I even have it when I'm jogging. It was pretty bad just now. Christ, it really threw me for a loop."

"I'm sure it must have."

"It's as if the earth . . . it's as if the goddamned *road* is reaching up for me. Jesus, that sounds awfully

strange, doesn't it, that sounds awfully, awfully
cuckoo—''

"Not at all, not at all, Mister—uh . . ." I was
coaxing him.

"I mean, it really drags me down, it *really* drags
me down, Mr. Harris, you can't imagine—"

He went on talking, babbling, really, for a good
five minutes. At one point he said, "It's probably
like being sucked back into the womb, don't you
think?"—and shivered visibly at the idea, as if he
had a chill. I listened, nodded occasionally, said
"Uh-huh" when I thought I should, and after a while
he seemed to wind down. He took a deep breath,
looked up, extended his hand, and smiled. "Thank
you, thank you very much, Mr. Harris, you've been
a great help." He stood and jogged off, south, past
the trailer which I'd assumed was abandoned. As he
passed it, a tall, stocky older woman dressed in a
tattered blue and white dress, white socks, what looked
like ankle-high sneakers, and a gray scarf thrown
over her shoulders came out of the trailer and watched
him. Even from a distance—and the trailer was a
good one hundred fifty feet away—some emotions
are easy to spot, and perhaps it wasn't so much that I
could read the woman's face at that distance as that I
could read the stiff set of her body, but I knew that
she was watching the jogger with undisguised hatred.

CHAPTER EIGHT

These are the things I remember fondly about Erika:
I remember that she liked to make love with her
socks on because her feet got cold. I remember that
she quickly learned the names of most of the birds
that came to feed at our feeding stations just west of
the house. She got a kick out of being able to name
them, as if their names, or her ability to remember
them, or both, involved the use of a whole different
language.

I remember that she did not like the dark. It was
not a matter of being *afraid* of it so much as simply

being uncomfortable with it. The only time we ever talked about it, she said she wasn't sure why it made her uncomfortable, and then she thought a moment and added, "I think that I *feel* too much in it, Jack. I feel that it's going to solidify," which mystified me.

She quite often mystifies me, which is something, of course, that people often do to other people. Sometimes it's a game; sometimes it's a pose; sometimes it's real. With Erika, it's real. She often mystifies herself, I think.

In March, for instance, she began to seek out the dark. First the night-light that she always kept burning in the bedroom got unplugged. Then the curtains, which I'd lately gotten into the habit of leaving open in order to let in what light there might be (except when I insisted that the heating bills would be lower if we closed them), got closed permanently, and the translucent shades behind them got replaced with opaque. And yet she still was uncomfortable.

I came up to the bedroom after working late and found her in a rocking chair, in the dark. I went over to her, put my hands on her shoulders, found that she was trembling. "Erika," I asked, "why are you trembling?"

"I don't know," she answered, her voice low, as if she didn't want to talk.

"Are you cold?"

"Yes. A little." She was whispering now. "I'm a little cold." She was dressed warmly enough, and the night wasn't particularly cold.

"Can I get you a blanket?"

She shook her head. "It wouldn't help. It's the dark."

"I don't understand." I was still leaning over her, my hands on her shoulders, which seemed to help because she stopped trembling. "What do you mean, 'It's the dark'? I'll turn the light on—"

"No," she cut in. "No. It's okay. It's nothing. The dark makes me cold, that's all." She put her hands on my forearms. She repeated, at a whisper, "The dark makes me cold."

I went to Granada the following morning. I had decided to take the day off because I'd worked a good twelve days straight, trying to meet the deadline on the Earth's-Way account that I realized, at last, wouldn't get met anyway. Erika had given me directions: "Down Route 64 to Clement Road," she said. "That's about two miles from East Cohocton."

"Yes," I said. "I know where it is."

"Good. You go about five miles down Clement Road, Jack. Maybe six miles. You'll see a sign that says 'Granada, Next Right.' When you go right, you've got another mile or so to go down this lousy dirt road—" She paused, continued, "God, I don't know why I went down it at all, Jack. I guess I was lucky I didn't break an axle. Some of those potholes are real killers—you'll find out."

I did find out. I had to keep my three-year-old Toyota well below twenty down that road to Granada.

The remains of a gate led into the place. It stood ten feet tall, and one side—which bore the letters GRAN—was lying in the road that led directly into Granada. The other side had the letters ADA on it.

From the gate, Granada looked much like a thousand similar bedroom communities. The houses were familiar pastel greens and pastel blues and pastel pinks. They were larger than most such houses, though not ostentatious, and were arranged in a nearly complete ring around a circular park that was all but totally overgrown by weeds and thickets crowding into the roadway.

I expected to see children playing, men pruning hedges, heads turning as a new and strange car entered the little community. But Granada was empty, and it had clearly been empty for more than a few years. It had the unmistakable patina of abandonment and decay about it. It smelled of the earth—which was shouldering back—not even faintly of car exhausts and driveway sealer and chemical fertilizer. And there were no noises of children or pets or stereos. Only the quick putta-putta of my Toyota, the high keening sound of the snow tires on the rutted blacktop. Nothing more. The place had a tense stillness to it, like a drawing done in hard, quick strokes with pen and ink.

I stopped the car in front of a big pastel blue house because its front door was standing open. I got out of the car, stared at the house a moment, expecting momentarily that a curtain would be drawn back slightly—there still were curtains in some of the windows—and that half a face would appear and disappear. But that didn't happen. If it had, it would have scared the hell out of me.

I saw an FBI warning poster nailed to the left of the front door, a pile of feces halfway up the concrete walkway to the house, an empty plastic Pepsi bottle in the yard to my left, and near it, a small black wheel, like a lawnmower wheel. The grass was matted, wet, and very short.

Along the edge of the walkway, there was a strip of mud six inches wide. I saw footprints in this mud.

I went to the front door of the house, stuck my head in, and said "Hello" several times. There was no answer. I could see the foyer, a part of the living room, an open dining area. Most of the furniture in these rooms had been removed, except for a pine kitchen chair lying on its side just ahead of me, in the foyer. The blue striped wallpaper was peeling from the top and the hardwood floors were wavy— here and there some of the boards stuck an inch or so above the level of the others. The ceiling, which had been done in swirls of a thick beige paint, was home for dozens and dozens of flies. Some wandered about, but most were still; and as I watched them, I became aware that I could smell them, faintly.

I went into the foyer, stopped, said "Hello" again. At the other side of the living room, directly opposite me, a huge picture window, intact, over-looked fields and woods behind the house.

I didn't think that anyone was living in the house. I thought it was possible that transients camped out in all the houses in Granada. "Is anyone here?" I said, and because I heard nothing except the low humming of the flies, I made my way into the living room.

A woman was asleep there. She was in a dark blue sleeping bag, her head on a green knapsack. She had short, dark blonde hair, and high cheekbones.

I said "I'm sorry," though she was still asleep, and started to back out of the room.

Her eyes fluttered open. She saw me, looked momentarily stunned, a little embarrassed. Then, as she sat up, a smile appeared on her thin, red lips. "I'm Sarah," she said, shrugged out of the sleeping bag, and stood. She was tall—almost six feet, I guessed—and gracefully thin. She was wearing a pair of gray overalls, a long-sleeved white cotton shirt with a turtleneck collar, and thick white socks; I saw a pair of Sorrel boots near the sleeping bag. She came over to me, her hand extended.

I took her hand. "Hi," I said. "I'm Jack Harris."

"Hello, Jack." She looked to be in her early forties, and surprisingly, considering the circumstances, had a distinct air of refinement about her. "You surprised me."

"Yes. I'm sorry." I glanced about, and grinned questioningly. "You don't live here, do you?"

She waved the question away. "No, Jack. Of course not. No, I live in Brighton." Thirty miles east of Rochester. "I come here from time to time. It's an interesting place, don't you think? Granada, I mean."

"Sure," I said, obviously unconvinced. "I suppose it is."

"You don't think so?" This seemed to surprise her. She stared silently at me a moment, then went back to her sleeping bag, rolled and tied it, and started to put her boots on. She said, as she laced one of them, "I've been coming here for several years, Jack." She thought a moment, looked quizzically at me. "I have permission, I mean, if you're someone who should be concerned about that."

I shook my head. "No. My wife told me about this place. She came by a couple of days ago."

"Yes," Sarah said. "I saw her car." She slipped the other boot on, began to lace it. "No one else comes here anymore. They used to, in the first couple of years, but no more. The novelty has worn off, I think."

"Oh?" I said.

She straightened, stuck her hands into the pockets of her overalls. "Uh-huh. And it suits me fine, Jack. I'd just as soon not be tripping over the tourists—that sounds crass, I know—"

"Sarah," I cut in, "I have no idea what you're talking about."

She looked at me. "Really?"

"Really."

She smiled. "Then you're something of a virgin, aren't you?" Her smile flattened. "It's pretty grim stuff, Jack, real *National Enquirer* I-ate-my-grandmother kind of stuff, and it's more than just a little depressing. I mean—people were not only *murdered* here—" She stopped, picked up her sleeping bag, and walked toward me. "Come on, Jack. I'll show you around the place. There's not much to see anymore but there's lots to tell—more, I think, than you'll probably want to hear."

"It sounds intriguing," I said, and followed her outside.

I think that people are beginning to drift back, now, to the village, to Cohocton. Occasionally, when I'm in the living room listening to music or waiting quietly for Erika, I see a furniture-laden pickup truck pass by, going toward the village, or a car loaded with people and belongings. I'm not sure what I think of this. I think it's sad, on the one hand, that a village should stand idle and empty. Villages are meant to be lived in, after all. But of course, Cohocton has never lacked for inhabitants.

And so I assume, when I see that people are coming back, that a season is done. And I assume that another has begun. I have no real way of knowing. It's a romantic notion, I think. Living with Erika has filled me with romantic notions.

That life continues, for instance. That there is a kind of vast reservoir of life beneath our feet and that everything living rises up from it, in one way or another—the mechanics of the thing aren't very important, only the fact that it happens—and then goes back after a while to the place where it started.

Toss a pail of water into the ocean. It doesn't *go* anywhere, of course, but out of that pail.

Erika used to have nightmares. She tells me they were nightmares from her childhood, and when she first started having them I told her I was surprised, that I thought, from the photographs and from what she'd told me, that her childhood had been pretty good. I asked her if her nightmares had to do with her parents' deaths and she said no, she didn't think so. She said they had to do with hunger, and with eating, with becoming engorged. That was the word she used. "I become engorged, Jack. And I drift. I drift away from . . . things. From events. From existence. And for a while I'm very happy."

"It sounds like limbo," I said.

She shook her head. "No. No, I think something happens, there. I think I grow there; I think I *grew* there," she corrected, apparently because she realized she'd been talking about dreams of her childhood.

"Then it's Freudian," I suggested. "It has to do with puberty, with growing up, and becoming a sexual being." I leered at her.

She chuckled softly, quickly. "It depends a lot on what I'm eating, doesn't it?"

I nodded. "Yes, it does."

Occasionally, she still has nightmares. She had one a couple of nights after I found her huddled in the darkness, and when I woke her from it—because she'd been moaning pitifully—she told me that it was a dream of hunger again. "But not the same kind of hunger, Jack," she added. "It's something else's hunger, I think. It's the earth's hunger."

I smiled at her; I touched her cheek—my way of trying to comfort her, because she clearly needed comforting. But I could say nothing because I have learned from her that silence is preferable to the comforting but meaningless phrase.

I hugged her instead. She hugged me. Eventually she stopped hugging me and went back to sleep.

It was some time later that night, several hours before dawn, that I was awakened by the sound of voices at a distance, as if a couple of moths were caught between the window and screen. I pushed myself up on my elbows, glanced at Erika, whose back was turned, and decided there was no point in waking her. I got out of bed, went to the window, drew the curtains. The road is a good three hundred feet from the house, and the night was nearly pitch-dark, but I found that if I looked up slightly from the level of the road, I could see random movement, as if people were walking there.

I opened the window and leaned forward, so my nose and cheek were touching the screen. I could hear the chorus of voices more clearly and I could make out individual voices, even an occasional string of words. I thought at first that I was seeing a line of Boy Scouts on some early morning hike because there was a Boy Scout camp not far off, certainly within hiking distance. Then I realized that the line was too ragged, that the voices were a mixture of male and female. And after all, Boy Scouts probably said very little when they were on a hike.

From the bed, Erika asked. "What are you doing, Jack?"

"Nothing," I answered. "I'm watching some people out there, some Boy Scouts, I think."

"It's cold, Jack. Come back to bed, okay?"

"In a moment." I could see the people on the road more clearly now. There were at least a dozen of them. Some seemed to be on the narrow path which led to Martin's house. "Friends of the guy across the road, I think."

"The Boy Scouts are friends of the guy across the road? What in the hell are you talking about, Jack?"

"I don't think they're Boy Scouts, Erika. Not really. I *thought* they were Boy Scouts . . ." It looked as if one of the people on the road had started wandering toward the house. "Jesus," I whispered.

"Come back to bed, Jack," Erika pleaded. "It's cold."

"In a few moments," I said. "I have to go downstairs. I'm hungry. I'm going to go get a snack."

"A snack?" I heard her fumble with the alarm clock. "You're going to get a snack at 4:00 in the morning?!"

"I won't be long. Really. Just a minute or two." I closed the window—quietly, because I didn't want whoever was wandering toward the house to hear me. I drew the curtains, went down to the library, then onto the porch. But when I looked, I saw no one. And I heard nothing. Only, from above, Erika pleading for me to come back to bed. I heard the word "cold" from her, again and again.

I pulled open the porch door, noisily—it was a very snug fit with the porch floor—stuck my head out, and said, "Hello? Is someone there?" I got no answer. I went out onto the porch steps. "I'm going to call the police," I said. "If there's someone out here, I'm going to call the police." Still nothing. I stayed on the porch steps a good ten minutes. Erika continued calling to me. I called back, several times, "I'll be up!" I didn't want to say too much, and I didn't want to stray too far from the front of the house.

It was a very still morning, and it came to me that if I listened hard enough, I could probably hear the trespasser because no one can stay absolutely quiet for long. So I listened. But I heard nothing, and because the morning was cold and I was tired, and I longed to be back in bed, I started getting angry. "Goddamnit!" I hissed. "This isn't funny anymore. I'm going inside, I'm going to call the police." And I went inside, into the living room, and stood just to the right of the big window.

A huge and elegant maple tree stands twenty-five feet in front of that window. If I waited long enough, maybe I'd see the trespasser step out from behind that tree and walk off. It didn't happen. And after several minutes I heard behind me:

"What the hell are you doing, Jack?"

It was Erika. I jumped a little; I hadn't heard her open the library door. I answered, "I'm waiting for someone to come out from behind that tree."

"Who? A Boy Scout?"

"There are no Boy Scouts, Erika . . . I mean, there are Boy Scouts, sure, but there are no Boy Scouts out there."

"Then what's the problem?" Her voice betrayed her irritation. "My God, Jack, it's 4:30 in the morning, and here you are standing at the window looking at the darkness."

"I saw *people* out there, Erika."

"Out where?" I heard her cross the room, felt her stop just behind me, so her gown was touching my hand.

I nodded at the maple tree. "Out there. Behind that tree. I think they're behind that tree."

"Come up to bed, Jack. It's cold; I want you to come back to bed."

"Soon, Erika. A few minutes—"

"Now, Jack."

"Erika, this is a matter of security here. Go on up; get an extra blanket. I'll be up before you know it."

"I need you, Jack. Please."

"In a *moment*, Erika; I think there's someone around the house. This is important, for Christ's sake!" I became aware that I could no longer feel her gown on my hand. I turned my head. She was gone.

I went up to the bedroom, switched the light on, found her sitting on the edge of the bed, hugging herself as if for warmth. "Erika?" I said. "Are you okay?"

"Just cold, Jack," she answered. "Come to bed, now. Please come to bed."

"You're very quick, aren't you?" I said. "I never realized you were so quick."

"Quick?"

"Yes. You move very quickly."

"I don't know what you're talking about, Jack. Come to bed. Turn off the light and come back to bed."

She'd been pleading with me for half an hour, I realized. And in bed, with her, was where I wanted to be, so I said, "Yes, I'm sorry, it's late," and I went to bed.

CHAPTER NINE

" 'Murders, mutilation, and mayhem,' Jack?" Erika was clearly upset. "This woman actually said that—what was her name?"

"Sarah."

"Sarah what?"

"Sarah Talpey."

"And she actually used that phrase? Was she trying to be funny?"

"I don't think so." We were folding laundry. Erika has shown me how to fold shirts at least two dozen times, but my hands never cooperate. I handed her the shirt I was trying to fold. "Could you do this, hon?"

She took it from me.

I said, "She wasn't trying to be funny, Erika. I think she was trying to . . . distance herself."

"From what?" Erika used quick, stiff, agitated movements to fold the shirt I'd given her.

"From that place. She spends a lot of time there—"

"She sounds perverse, Jack."

I shook my head, made a production of folding a pair of my boxer shorts. "She's not perverse. Her brother was killed there—"

She cut in, looking suddenly very smug, "No one named Talpey died at Granada, Jack."

"Talpey is her married name, Erika."

Her look of smugness quickly dissipated. She grabbed a pair of socks, stuffed one into the other. I nodded at them. "That's how *I* fold socks, and you yell at me for it." I paused. "How did you know that no one named Talpey died in Granada, Erika?"

She lowered her head, shook it briskly. "We'll talk," she said.

"I hope so," I said.

But we never did.

This is what Sarah Talpey told me about Granada.

She told me that a dozen or more people died there, that several of the houses were burned, apparently to destroy evidence, and that several of the victims had been mutilated and cannibalized. "It happens in the best of cultures," she said. "I guess people get sick of the same old meat and potatoes."

And she told me that the case still was open, after twenty years. "Of course, no one cares much anymore. It's old news, and I guess there are bigger fish to fry these days. But it intrigues the hell out of me, Jack."

I told her that was obvious. She made the revelation that her brother had died in Granada. "I was doing postgraduate work at Barnard College then. I remember that someone from the FBI called and told me, point-blank, 'I'm sorry, Miss Gellis'—that was my maiden name—'but your brother's been killed. We'll need you to identify the body. Et cetera, et cetera. Norm was quite a bit older than I. And I'm the first to admit that the world has produced nicer people. But I cried a lot in the next couple of weeks, not merely because he was dead, but because he died that way. He was one of those who was cannibalized. Not completely, of course. That would hardly have left anything to identify, would it?" She took a breath. "Anyway, I started coming here, as a naturalist, several years ago." She smiled as if in apology. "That requires an explanation, I know. Why would a naturalist be interested in this place? And actually, it's not so much that I'm interested in the houses themselves as much as I'm interested in what *visited* them." Another pause. Another grin of apology. "Do you understand that, Jack?"

I shook my head.

"Of course you don't. And I probably sound like I'm not all there, right—the eccentric, bucolic naturalist?'' I grinned. She grinned back. ''No, Jack. I'm smart, I'm tough, and I'm pragmatic.'' She looked away, seemed lost in thought a moment, then continued, ''And when I dig into the earth I find . . . *life!*'' She looked up at me, smiled broadly. ''I find life, Jack. Do you understand that?''

''Yes,'' I said.

''Yes,'' she said. ''I think you do. I can tell that you do. And I'm glad you do, because that means we can talk. Later.''

''Later?''

''Come back here when you can. You'll find me. We'll talk. I'll tell you what's on my mind.'' And then she said good-bye, got into her bright red Chevy Lux 4×4 pickup, and drove off at a speed that my Toyota could never have maintained on that road.

We did talk; we talked quite a lot, and I learned much from her. I still do.

Our problems with moles stopped late in March, when the air turned bitterly cold.

We found one morning that some of the old copper water pipes had frozen. I had to creep around on my belly in the crawl space in the cellar, blow-dryer in hand, find the offending pipes, and thaw them.

One of our cats, Ginger, got herself lost around this time, too. I tromped through the woods, calling for her, several days in a row, with no luck, and at last decided that she'd either been picked up by someone or killed by a raccoon or a fox, or by one of the dozens of stray dogs that roamed the area—they always kept at a distance, so what we heard of them were only occasional barks and long howls. The most painful possibility was that she had frozen to death. This bothered me a lot because she was a creature who dearly loved warmth.

It bothered Erika, too, though she'd never seemed to like Ginger much, had always seemed merely to tolerate her. "She's a cat, Jack. Cats don't freeze to death," she said, but it was a question more than a statement.

"Sure they do, Erika, if it gets cold enough."

She spent the next three days on long, lone hikes through our woods, calling for Ginger. She didn't find her. And for the next couple of weeks she said to me now and again, "My God, Jack, I hope she didn't freeze to death," and I said to her that it was okay, that if she had, it was probably one of the best ways to die. But Erika didn't seem to understand that.

Late in March we went to the antique shop that the Alnors operated in their white barn. We were looking for a settee to put in the big, open room at the top of the stairs—we'd put some plants there, and a red beanbag chair (we could think of nowhere else to put it), an aquarium, and we'd decided at last to start giving it a *look* of some kind, *ambiance*. We'd seen a sturdy late-Victorian settee there on a previous visit, had priced it, and said that we hoped it would be there when we came back—although we had no plans to go back soon. The Alnors had nodded and smiled and said they thought it would be there, that business was not too good in the winter.

But it was gone. "A nice young couple bought it," Mr. Alnor told us. "Right after you looked at it, in fact."

The shop was incredibly cluttered, the aisles narrow, the atmosphere stiff and businesslike. Signs here and there warned that "Children must be accompanied by an adult." One sign proclaimed, "You break it, you bought it!" Another: "We'd like to keep your friendship—Don't ask for credit!" And there was the stiffly smiling presence of one of the Alnors at all times. "Just let us know how we can help you" was their line.

When we got to the shop that afternoon late in March there were several other people there: an older, well-dressed couple who walked arm in arm through the aisles, and what sounded like a family above us, on the barn's second floor, where furniture was kept. We could hear the slow clop-clop of several pairs of feet and the quicker, frantic noises of children. Noise seemed to carry well through the simple plank flooring above us, and the sounds of the children clearly upset Mrs. Alnor, who crossed her arms, grimaced, and said to her husband, "What do you suppose they're *doing* up there, Harry?"

Then we heard "Mommy?" very faintly from upstairs. I looked toward the stairway because I'd sensed a kind of tense urgency in the word.

Mrs. Alnor said again, "What do you suppose they're doing up there, Harry?"

And Harry said, "I'll go and see."

"Mommy?!" we heard again. Then, a second later, "Joyce?" It was a man's voice.

I felt Erika grab my arm. "Jack," she whispered, "something's wrong."

"Joyce?" we heard again. "What's wrong? Tell me what's wrong."

Mr. Alnor started for the stairs then. I followed. Erika followed me, her hand still on my arm.

"For God's sake, Joyce," we heard. "What in the hell are you doing?"

"Mommy?!"

"Get *out* of there, Joyce!"

"Harry," Mrs. Alnor said, "don't go up there, Harry."

He glanced incredulously around at her. I yelled up the stairs, "Is something wrong?"

"It's okay," the man yelled back. "This is our problem; we'll deal with it."

And that's when Harry Alnor vaulted up the stairs. I heard him, moments later: "What's she doing in there, mister?" The words were spoken with tight anger. A brief pause, then: "Come on out of there, young woman; you'll break it."

Erika and I went up. We stopped at the top of the stairs. I felt her grip on my arm strengthen, heard her whisper tremblingly, "Why's she doing that?"

Joyce—an attractive, dark-haired woman in her late twenties, I guessed, who was dressed in jeans and sneakers, a blue shirt, and denim vest—had crawled into a tall and very narrow cupboard, had gotten into a fetal position in it, and was looking very fearfully out from it at her husband and her daughter and at Harry Alnor.

She was whispering something, too. I couldn't hear her words, but I could read her lips. She was whispering, "The dark!" over and over again.

It bothered the hell out of Erika. The woman eventually got out of the cupboard, of course, and was led, trembling, from the antique shop to her car.

But Erika and I stayed a few minutes. Erika seemed confused, at odds with herself, caught at the verge of weeping, or laughing. Harry Alnor noticed it.

"Jesus Christ, mister," he said to me, nodding at Erika, "what the hell is wrong with *her*, now?"

"Please," I said, "don't use that tone."

"Give them room, Harry," Mrs. Alnor said.

We were at the doorway. I had my arm around Erika, who still was staring at the spot where Joyce's car had been. She'd said nothing since we were upstairs in the shop. "Why's she doing that?" she'd said then, several times. Now she said, "Why'd she do that, Jack?"

"She was confused," I said.

"She was nuts out of her head," said Harry Alnor.

"Shut up!" said Mrs. Alnor.

"Don't tell *me* to shut up, woman!"

And Erika said, "Please, let's go home, Jack." And we did.

*   *   *

I lost track of her that evening. She was in the spare room, rummaging through some boxes that were labeled MISC. JUNK, which meant only that whatever was in them was unimportant. I was in bed, reading an old Stephen King story, had lost myself in the world of Jody Verrel—who became one with the green stuff from a meteorite—and I heard Erika call, "Jack, come here, please." I heard nothing urgent in her tone. I supposed that she wanted me to help her move some boxes, so I called back, "In a moment."

I finished the King story, got up and went to the spare room. It's cluttered there. Besides the unpacked boxes, there are empty boxes, empty suitcases, photographic gear—from a time when I had a passionate, if short-lived, love for amateur photography—clothes baskets, an ironing board. It's a large, L-shaped room. The lower part of the L is short and narrow, and there are rough, handmade bookcases there, with odds and ends on them.

I paused in the doorway to the room. The bare overhead light was on, so it was bright enough that I could see most of the room, though not the far corner, and not, of course, the lower part of the L. "Erika? You rang?"

Nothing.

"Erika? Are you in here?"

Nothing.

I shrugged, guessed that she was downstairs, went to the top of the stairs, called to her, got no reply.

I saw that the door to the stairway was closed. I called louder, "Erika, are you down there?" heard nothing, cursed, went back to the spare room.

She was there. She was leaning over a box, some photographs in hand—some of the photographs that I have, now. When I came in, she looked up, bemused: "What are you doing, Jack?"

"I was looking for you," I told her.

"I've been right here."

"No. Not a few minutes ago."

She looked silently at me. Her look of bemusement changed to one of quick confusion; she said, "Sure I was." She straightened, crossed the room, showed me the photographs. "This," she explained, "was taken when I was ten or eleven." She pointed to the boy beside her. "His name was Timothy." She handed me the photograph. "Keep it, Jack. I want you to have it."

I shrugged. "But I have *you*, Erika."

"Of course you do, but take it, anyway. Please." I took it. She seemed pleased. She showed me another one: "And this is me with my mother . . ."

CHAPTER TEN

The following morning I had to go into the cellar once more, blow-dryer in hand, because the pipes leading to the kitchen faucets had frozen again. They freeze easily if the temperature dips into the teens or lower—the foundation directly in front of them is cracked, allowing cold air to focus on them.

Though it was easy to figure out which pipes were frozen, getting to them was another matter entirely. They're at the far end of a long, two-foot-tall crawl space which has a dirt floor and a ceiling that's alive with insects and spiders. The whole area smells strongly of sewage, too. (I vowed to have that smell checked out when I first went into the crawl space, but I never did.) And there were no lights in the crawl space, so it was necessary to creep along on my elbows and knees, a flashlight in one hand, blow-dryer in the other—attached to a thirty-foot-long extension cord—while I tried hard not to bang my head on the joists above.

When I got to the frozen pipes, I could see daylight through the inch-wide crack in the foundation. I could see, too, that someone was on the other side of the foundation, looking in.

I said, "Hello," surprised not only because I'd found someone looking at me but because I'd actually said hello to him.

He said "Hello" to me. His voice was a high tenor and very friendly.

"What are you doing?" I asked.

"What?" he said.

I repeated, louder, "What are you doing?"

He answered, "I don't know."

This bothered me. I said nothing for a few moments because I could think of nothing to say. At last I asked him, "Who are you?"

He didn't answer.

"Could you tell me who you are?" I shouted.

From within the house I heard Erika yell, "What'd you say, Jack?"

I turned my face to the ceiling of the crawl space. "Nothing," I yelled. "Stay in the house, Erika!" I turned back to the crack in the foundation. I saw that more of the light coming through was obscured. "What are you doing?" I said to the man there.

"I'm sticking my fingers in," he answered.

"Don't do that," I said, paused, went on, "Why are you doing that?"

"I don't know," he answered.

"Don't stick your fingers in there," I said again, and turned to the ceiling of the crawl space. "Erika, stay in the house. Lock the doors."

The man outside the foundation said, "I can't get them out." He didn't sound bothered or upset. He was merely making a statement of fact. "My fingers are stuck."

"Please," I said loudly, "get your fingers *out* of there."

He said nothing.

"What did you stick your fingers in there for in the first place?"

Nothing.

"Are you still there?" I asked. It was a stupid question. I could see clearly enough that he was there.

"Yes," he said.

"Will you wait there?"

"I don't know."

"I'm asking you to wait there. Please."

He said nothing.

I watched him. I could see little—the suggestion of an eye, some dark skin, the center of a pair of dark, full lips, and beyond him, the trunk of our crab apple tree. At last I said, "Wait there. I'm coming out. Please wait there."

"I don't know," he said.

I started backing out of the crawl space. From within the house, Erika called, "What's wrong, Jack? Is something wrong?"

"Stay inside, Erika!" I yelled.

"Jack, I think there's someone outside the house!"

"Stay inside, damnit!" I was halfway back to the cellar proper now, and Erika's voice was growing indistinct. "Erika?" I yelled.

She yelled back. I couldn't understand her. I yelled, "Erika, call the police!" I heard nothing from her.

I was at the cellar door now. I pulled it open, ran up the short flight of stone steps, looked to my left, where the man should have been. I saw no one.

Erika appeared seconds later. She looked quizzically at me.

"Jack, there was someone out here. There was a man out here."

"Yes," I said, "I talked to him."

I found some footprints in the mud near the crack in the foundation and I followed them to where the underbrush took over a hundred feet west of the house. I pushed into the underbrush, hollered, "Is anyone there?" I waited a moment, then added, "Are you there?" But I got no response, and when I turned to go back to the house, I found that Erika was just behind me.

"Jack," she said, "when you were in the cellar, did you tell me to call the police?"

I nodded. "Yes. I did."

"I thought so." She gestured vaguely toward the road far in front of the house and said, as if embarrassed, "They told me they'd be here in five minutes."

The cop who came was named Larry Whipple. He was dressed in overalls and an orange hunting jacket, and he explained that he never wore "that dumb police uniform" unless he had to, and since it was his day off—"But I still monitor the calls, you know"—he figured he didn't have to.

He was a big man, just on the unhealthy side of chubby. He had a long, full face, a short black beard and mustache, and small, wide-set eyes. He was in his late forties, I guessed. His black hair was thinning severely.

I showed him into the kitchen, asked him to sit down. He pulled a chair out, sat, got a notepad from one pocket of his hunting jacket and a pencil from another. "So, what seems to be the problem here?" He licked the end of the pencil, held it poised against a page of the notepad. I got the clear idea that he wasn't terribly bright.

"The problem is," I began and sat down across from him, "trespassers."

He wrote it in the notepad. It took him a while; he seemed to have trouble with the spelling. Finally, he looked up, grinned, looked down again, underlined the word, looked up once more, grinned yet again. He had very straight, white teeth. "What sorts of trespassers, Mr. Harris?"

"What sorts?" I asked. Erika came and sat down between us at the circular table. "I don't understand."

"Well." He held his hand up and touched the index finger of his right hand to the fingers of his left. "There's Number One: your hunting trespasser, and they're thicker than flies on cow shit. Then there's Two: your basic hiking type; you know, some asshole from the city, wants to walk in the woods and can't read signs. Then there's Number Three: the squatter type."

"The squatter type?" Erika asked.

Whipple nodded sagely. "Only a few a those, and I can name most of 'em, but I don't think you got any or I'd know about it." He paused, scribbled something on the notepad, continued, "In fact, we got a whole mess a squatters down south of Cohocton, near the Ononda Creek. They built shacks, maybe thirty of 'em, it's kind of a little community, you know, a little village, and we call it the Oxbow, I don't know why." He stopped again. "But it wouldn't be none of those people 'cuz they pretty much stay right where they are, 'specially this time a the year 'cuz it's not real warm yet, you know. What kind you got? You think it was a hunter?"

I shook my head. "No. I don't think so. I don't think he was carrying a gun."

"Uh-huh." He gestured to indicate the outdoors.
"I saw all your No Hunting signs, and I guess you
got the right to put 'em up, but you ain't gonna make
no friends that way 'cuz we all—most of us, anyway—
we all hunt, we been huntin' most our lives, practi-
cally—"

"That's neither here nor there, is it?" Erika broke
in.

"Huh?" he said, obviously confused.

"Our No Hunting signs aren't what's at issue,
right?" I said.

He shrugged. "I guess not."

"The man who was *trespassing* is the issue,"
Erika said. "That's why we called you."

Larry Whipple nodded slowly. "Yes. That's right.
That's why I'm here." He smiled broadly. "So tell
me about him."

"About the trespasser?"

His smile broadened even further. "Yes, Mr. Harris,
about the trespasser."

"Okay," I said, feeling suddenly defensive and
ill-at-ease, "I'll tell you about him." But I could tell
him precious little, of course, only that the man was
dark-skinned, but not black, and that his eyes were
probably dark, that he'd gotten his fingers stuck in
the crack in the foundation, and that he hadn't waited
around, though I'd asked him to. Larry Whipple
thought this was funny. "These trespassers usually
don't do precisely what you tell them to do, Mr.
Harris," he said, chuckling. Then he stood, stuck his

notepad into the pocket of his hunting jacket, and said, at the door, "No, it's okay, I'll see myself out," though neither of us had stood. Then he left.

I turned to Erika. She had a look of puzzlement on her face. I said to her, "Erika, what in the hell do you suppose that was all about?"

She shrugged. "I guess he didn't want to help us, Jack."

CHAPTER ELEVEN

We went into Cohocton several evenings later. Neither of us wanted to cook that night, and since we both enjoyed a submarine sandwich that was made well—mine with lots of mayonnaise, oil, and cheese, and Erika's with several inches of onions over lean meat—we decided to go to a place called Jack's Subs and Pizza. It was at the north end of Cohocton's main street, past three of the five hardware stores in town, a drugstore, Buckles, Boots & Buttons, a used clothing store, the First National Bank of Cohocton, a laundromat, an ''Art Gallery'' that exhibited the works of local artists almost exclusively (some of whom were quite good, though there were the usual frowning clowns, aged barns, and stylized owls), a privately owned IGA store, the Cohocton Diner, and the Cohocton Hotel, a rambling Victorian monstrosity that had been renovated fifty years earlier to give its cavernous interior a gaudy art-deco look.

As usual in the evening, Cohocton was all but deserted. A few battered pickup trucks were parked on Main Street, one in front of the bank, two in front of C. R. Boring Hardware. A thin, aged man I had come to know only as Knebel, pronounced "neeble," was out walking his old, fat German shepherd, Hans.

I stopped in front of Jack's Pizza and Subs; Erika and I got out of the car. I nodded at Knebel, who was across the street; he nodded back, brought Hans up short on the leash. "Shit," I whispered, because I realized that Knebel wanted to talk. He liked to talk. He lived alone, in a grim, two-room apartment behind the Middletown Tavern, on North Main Street, and had no living relatives or close friends. That was why, I'd been told, he latched onto newcomers and chewed their ears off.

He crossed the street, Hans in tow. In the middle of the street the dog decided to sit down; he coaxed it with a few soothing words and pats on the head and the dog got going.

"Hi, Knebel," I called.

Erika, beside me, asked, "Who's he?"

I turned to her, whispered, "No one. I won't be long. Why don't you go in and get the subs?"

She shrugged, said "Sure," and went inside.

Knebel finished crossing the street and stuck his hand out to me. I took it. "Hi, Knebel," I said again.

"Jack," he said, "it's good to see you." He nodded at the sub shop. "Getting some subs?"

I nodded.

"Give the little woman some time off, eh?" He nodded in agreement with himself. He was a painfully thin man, with a full head of bright white hair, a large skull, big, flat eyes, and a broad mouth; he reminded me of a huge, white lollypop that's had a face painted on it. He nodded again, still in agreement with himself, and added, "It's a good way to keep 'em in line, Jack."

"I don't think that way, Knebel," I said, and was surprised that it sounded like an apology.

"Uh-huh." He nudged my arm with his elbow. "Don't stick around too long in town tonight, Jack."

This took me by surprise. "Sorry?" I said.

"We've got some trouble here tonight." He nodded, again in self-agreement.

"I don't understand. What kind of trouble?"

He turned, patted the German shepherd's head, turned back to me. "I'm not sure. I saw some things." He stopped.

"What kind of things?" I coaxed.

"People," he answered, and gestured with his arm toward the laundromat, several hundred feet away on the other side of the street. "There," he went on, and nodded at the Cohocton Hotel, on our side of the

street and a block further down from the laundromat.
"There, too."

I felt a smile start on my lips; I suppressed it.
"What's the significance, Knebel?" I asked.

"People," he repeated with emphasis, "standing
by themselves, Jack. In the dark." He paused
meaningfully, then repeated, "People standing by
themselves, in the dark."

"Doing what?" I asked.

"Nothing."

"And?"

"That's it." He looked confused. "Isn't it enough?"

I didn't know what to say. I shrugged.

"This is a little town," he said.

"Yes, it is."

"I know everyone. And they know me. You want
significance? *That's* the significance."

Erika appeared from the sub shop, a white sandwich bag in each hand. She stopped halfway down
the steps and looked confusedly at me. "I think he
should have marked these, Jack," she said. "I don't
know which one's yours."

"The greasy one," I said.

Knebel said, nodding at Erika, "So you get her
home and safe quick's you can, okay?"

I sighed. "I'll do that, Knebel."

"I'd say that'd be the best thing tonight, Jack."
He nodded in self-agreement, tugged on the German
shepherd's leash, and walked stiffly off, toward North
Main Street.

*　　*　　*

Tall walnut and maple trees crowded both sides of the narrow road from Cohocton to the house, and on this night, the smell of wood smoke—from houses that used wood stoves—was heavy and unpleasant, in spots nearly like a fog. No one walked this road at night—not, I think, because it was dangerous but because the people who lived in the area drove if they had someplace to go.

That evening, when we were still a mile or so from home, Erika said, "I could stay here a long time, Jack." I heard something deeply meaningful in her voice, and something tense, too, as if she were afraid of what she was saying.

"Me, too," I said.

I felt her hand on mine on the steering wheel, and I glanced at it, surprised. When I looked up, I saw a deer running along the right-hand side of the road about fifty yards ahead of the car. I had already learned that the deer ran in groups of three or four—if one got caught in the glare of headlights, the chances were very good that another, and another, and another would quickly follow. So I hit the brakes. "Hold on!" I said to Erika, and found suddenly that the car was facing the right side of the road, its high beams hard on the trees there. I cursed, let off the brakes; the car straightened. I pumped the brakes, brought the car to a halt, took a breath, studied the road ahead. The deer I'd braked for was a good hundred yards off now. As I watched, it angled sharply to the left, across the road, and was gone. Another deer appeared seconds later, then another.

Erika said, "I saw someone standing next to the road, Jack."

I glanced at her. "Oh?"

She nodded; she was looking straight ahead. "Yes, when the car skidded."

I glanced back through the rear window and saw the deep red glow of the brake lights on darkness, nothing else. I put the car in park, took my foot off the brake, saw the gray suggestion of sky, a black horizon. I noticed the smell of the wood smoke, too, and it got me thinking about house fires and carbon monoxide poisoning.

Erika said, "But he belongs here."

"Does he?"

She nodded again.

I asked, "He lives here, Erika?"

"Sure," she answered.

I put the car in drive, touched the accelerator; the car moved very slowly forward—the deer had spooked me and I was being extra cautious. I said, "How do you know all that, Erika?"

"Because I've seen him before."

I caught the suggestion of movement a hundred feet ahead, near the side of the road, and I slowed the car to a crawl.

"Where?" I asked.

"Near the house," she answered. "The other morning. When you were in the cellar."

I glanced quickly at her. "You're kidding." I glanced back. The thing at the side of the road appeared; it was a big raccoon. It ambled several feet into the road, got caught in the full glare of the headlights, loped back to the shoulder, and hesitated there, as if agitated by the presence of the car.

"No," Erika said. "It was the same man. He was wearing the same clothes."

The raccoon got up on its haunches, then down on all fours, and scooted across the road. I said to Erika, "You never told me you knew what the man was wearing. That's important stuff."

She shook her head. "No, it isn't, Jack. He belongs here."

I sighed. "Are you saying we've got goofy neighbors, Erika?"

"I thought you knew we had goofy neighbors, Jack." I heard wry amusement in her voice and realized that it signaled a clear change in her tone. "Everybody's got goofy neighbors," she declared. "I'm sure that *we're* someone's goofy neighbors."

"Uh-huh," I said, "sure we are," and I pushed the accelerator halfway to the floor. The car shot forward, giving me a little rush of excitement. "The hell with the damned deer," I muttered.

"And the hell with goofy neighbors!" Erika said aloud. "I'm hungry!"

She has a strange sense of humor. It's unpredictable, a little perverse, and she delights in the absurd. She has a Kliban poster in the music room. It shows a barrel-bodied, huge-headed pen-and-ink cat with a shit-eating grin on its mouth, and a scrawny mouse under its paw. "Love to eat them mousies," the cat's saying; "bite they little heads off."

When she got the poster, she explained simply—"That cat's honest." She grinned lopsidely. "I like honesty."

CHAPTER TWELVE

I found myself back in Granada several days later. I'm uncertain what drew me there, because it was a strange and depressing place and it made me more than a little uncomfortable (the same way, I remembered, that I'd felt when I visited France five years earlier and didn't speak the language, like being blind and in a room whose dimensions are unknown).

It might have been Sarah Talpey who drew me back because the things she'd said, and the way she'd said them, had posed more questions than they'd answered. Or I simply could have been bored, alone at the house (it was a Monday, and Erika always put in at least twelve hours at her shop on Mondays).

Sarah was in Granada that day. It was a bright, warm morning, the first week in April, and when I got out of the car a hornet buzzed me once, and again, then found the interior of the car and got stuck there. I cursed, closed the door, decided to deal with it later.

I was in front of the pastel blue house where I'd discovered Sarah. She was just coming out of it, dressed in gray overalls, a white shirt, and a blue ski jacket opened at the front. She was carrying something under her right arm. She smiled, waved, said, "Hello. Jack, isn't it?"

"Yes," I said loudly. "Hi."

She came quickly down the battered walkway, extended her free hand; I took it. "I'm Sarah," she said. "Remember?"

"I remember."

She let go of my hand, noticed that I was looking at the thing she was carrying under her arm. She said, "I found this today," and held it out for me to see. It was a tattered brown suede jacket. She turned her head slightly, nodded, "In that house, in the attic. Under the insulation."

It was a child's jacket, that was obvious, and it was torn in several places. Around the collar it looked as if it might have been chewed.

Sarah went on, "It's a marvelous find, Jack. It belonged to one of the children who lived here—a boy named Robin." She held up the jacket's right sleeve. The name Robin had been sewn there in red thread. "Robin Graham," she went on, and tucked the jacket back under her arm. "He was eleven years old. A twin, I think. I'll have to check that. And he turned up missing one day." A flat, sad grin appeared on her lips. "He was never found. Lots and lots of people looked for him, and for quite a long time, too. Then his brother turned up missing, too, and *he* was never found, and things got pretty frantic. But that was just the tip of the iceberg, I'm afraid."

"Oh?" I said.

She nodded. "Uh-huh." She lifted her head, closed her eyes briefly, opened them, and smiled. "God, what a day, Jack!" She took my elbow. "C'mon, walk with me."

I spent several hours with her in Granada that morning. We did a lot of walking, more than I'd done in some time (my legs ached the next day from it), and she went into detail about Granada, why she was there, what had happened twenty years ago. And when she was done and was walking me to my car, I told her that she had scared the hell out of me.

"Good," she said.

"I don't believe a word of it, Sarah, but I enjoy a good story well told."

She smiled thinly, opened my car door. "So do I, Jack," she said, leaned over and looked into my car. "I'll get that hornet out for you. I think you're probably a little squeamish about that sort of thing."

"Thanks," I said. "I am."

* * *

Once, on a business trip to New York City, I had to spend an hour or so at Grand Central Station. I found that all the stories I'd heard about it were true. It's crowded, it's noisy, it's smelly, most of the people are rude, the cops surly. And it does not lack for crazies. There are probably a hundred or more crazies there at any given time. Usually, they're benign and predictable—people who carry on long and unintelligible conversations with themselves, people who wander aimlessly from place to place, people who accuse passersby of all kinds of immorality. But on this particular business trip I ran into a very rare type of crazy, the Imaginative and Articulate Crazy. He was a man in his late forties who called himself "The Late Dr. Bernie Swan." He was dressed very stylishly, looked as if he had money, and for a full hour and a half he told me, in wonderful detail, about the giant spiders that lived in Manhattan's subway system. He explained that they were "a heavily mutated species of arachnid and they subsist almost entirely on a diet of subway freeloaders." I found myself vastly entertained, and when he was finished I said that he should try writing novels or short stories. He shook his head slowly and seriously—he was a distinguished-looking man with a well-groomed black mustache, nicely coiffed hair, intelligent gray eyes—and said, "No, I'm afraid not. Those sorts of people deal in fiction, you see," then stood and strode off, to the Forty-second Street exit, his gait quick and purposeful, as if he had places to go and people to see.

When I drove home after spending the morning with Sarah Talpey, I thought about him and his "heavily mutated arachnids," and I wondered if Sarah, too, got a big kick out of the stories she told, and if she believed them, as well. I remember hoping she did because I had grown to like her and I didn't want to believe she was bringing herself unhappiness.

"The earth produced us all," she told me. "I believe that, Jack. Do you believe that?"

"Sure," I said, though I had little idea what she was talking about.

"The earth and air and sunlight produced us all," she said. We were walking several hundred feet north of Granada on a narrow path. It was a deer path, she explained; as she talked she kept her hands folded behind her, Robin Graham's brown suede jacket tucked under her arm. She held her head down, wore a little frown. She is a very attractive woman, and I couldn't help looking at her often as she spoke, though she rarely looked at me. I got the idea that she was delivering a monologue. She went on, "The earth and air and sunlight produce all kinds of things, Jack."

"Uh-huh," I said.

She turned her head and gave me a quick, embarrassed grin. "That wasn't awfully profound, was it?"

I said nothing.

She turned back. "It's at the heart of all this, though."

"All this?"

She gestured obliquely with her free arm. "Yes. Granada."

"It is?" I heard the incredulity in my voice.

"Yes—Jack, do you want to know what really happened here? Twenty years ago." She didn't give me a chance to answer; she hurried on, as if in a sudden frenzy, "The earth *reared* up, Jack, and caught those people with their pants down. The *earth* swept them away. The earth produced its own"—she swung her arm wide—"and swept them away. *Swept* them away. Robin Graham, my brother—*all* of them." She paused. Then she whispered, "They were swept away."

"By arms of loving grace," I said.

She looked momentarily confused. "Maybe," she said. "I don't know. Maybe."

"And I don't know what we're talking about, Sarah."

"Arms of loving grace. That's important, Jack."

"Is it?"

She nodded once, earnestly, but said nothing.

I asked, "Why is it?"

"Because we all come from the earth, Jack. And we all go back to it. So you see, there's no real difference between us and them."

"Oh? Who's them?"

Again she gestured behind her. "The ones who visited Granada twenty years ago."

"And did what?"

"And did what you see there." She sounded annoyed.

"Are you telling me you know who they were?"

"Yes."

"By name?"

"No. That's not relevant."

"Oh?"

"The earth doesn't give her children names, Jack. *We* do that. The earth does what it does. It produces."

"And what does the earth produce? Precisely."

"It produces people. Like you and me and my brother Norm and Robin Graham."

"But those are real people, and they have real names." I realized that I was humoring her and I didn't like it.

She grinned quickly, impatiently. "Yes, of course they do," she said. "Everyone has names." I got the idea, then, that she had begun humoring *me*. "People are given names. Or they take them. And they live with them, are known by them, and die with them."

"You're being awfully cryptic."

"No, I'm not. Listen to me. The things I'm telling you are true."

We got to the end of the deer path, and hesitated. I said to her, before we turned and started back, "But you haven't told me anything, Sarah."

"I've told you that the earth produces, and I've told you what it produces, and what happened here, Jack. Listen to me."

But I didn't listen to her. I didn't listen to several

people. Like Harry Simms, for instance, when he swept out of the woods and screamed that he couldn't breathe. I thought he was nuts. I thought he was playing a game. How was I to know what was happening to him?

And I didn't listen to Erika, either. Not closely enough, anyway, not in the way I should have listened to her. It wouldn't have made any difference, after all. Once the pail of water is thrown, you can't recall it. But I could have helped her through it, I could have eased her agony somehow.

And I didn't listen to my mother, either, although the knowledge she had was amorphous, little bits and pieces of suspicion that I doubt she'd ever have added up to anything meaningful.

It all adds up, now.

CHAPTER THIRTEEN

The master bedroom here at the house is big and rectangular, with high ceilings and two tall multi-paned windows, kitty-corner to each other (one has a southern exposure; the other faces west), a huge walk-in closet, and light green walls. It once had a fireplace on the north wall, but it was plastered over, so only its outlines show. Residue from the oil heat has collected in front of the wall studs, where concentrations of moisture attracted it—so, on certain days, the green walls look as if very faint gray bars have been painted on them.

Erika never liked this room. She says that she feels uncomfortable in it, trapped in it—I never understood why—so, after a while, I grew accustomed to waking very early and finding that she was not in the bed, that she'd gone into the guest room to sleep or into the music room, which has a cot in it and is warmer than the guest room, anyway.

The night after I talked to Sarah I woke at a little past 2:00 and found that Erika was not in the bed with me. I wanted her in the bed with me; I needed her with me. So I got up and went looking for her. I looked in the guest bedroom first. It's down the hall from the master bedroom. I opened the door, peeked in, and even in the dim light filtering through the heavy curtains from a spotlight over the side porch—which we kept burning for safety's sake—I knew that the room was empty. I said, anyway, "Erika?" and flicked the overhead light on. The room was empty, the bed untouched. I went downstairs to the music room, found that it was empty, too. I cursed. "Erika?" I called. "Erika, where are you?" I got no answer. I decided that I had better make a search of the house.

I found her in the dining room, seated at the head of the table, in the captain's chair, with her back to the large window that looks out on the side yard and the woods beyond. She'd drawn the curtains open on this window. And when I flicked the light on, she said, "No, keep it off, Jack," so I turned it off. She gestured with her head toward the window. "Look out there."

I looked. The spotlight over the side porch was

lighting the whole area nicely. I could see our three crab apple trees—the closest had a distinct whitish cast to it, from the spotlight—and our bird feeders (two of which are miniature houses on long steel "squirrel proof" poles), the small gray picnic table that we'd brought from Syracuse, the aged wooden bridge over the narrow creek. I could see the tufted, hulking suggestion of the woods beyond, as well, and above them the belt of the constellation Orion, just barely visible in the glare of the spotlamp.

I said to Erika, "I'm looking. What am I supposed to see?"

She turned in her chair, stared out the window for several seconds, turned back. "Oh," she said, her voice low and apologetic, "they're gone."

"They are?"

"Yes."

She stood. She was dressed in a sheer black floor-length nightgown that I'd gotten her for Christmas, and as she drew the curtains shut and the light from the spotlamp hit her, it came to me in a rush just why I'd gotten out of bed to find her. "You look awfully sexy, Erika," I said.

"Do I?" she said. "Thanks. You can turn on the light now."

"Uh-huh. But then, you always look sexy, of course." I flicked the light on.

"Of course."

I went over to her, put my hands on her waist. "What was out there?" I ran my hands slowly up and down her torso; my palms touched and lingered on her breasts.

"Deer," she answered, and paused for several seconds. "People, maybe."

I moved back from her a step, my hands on her waist. "People?" I said. "You mean the snowmobilers?"

She shook her head slightly; a little smile appeared on her mouth, as if she were vaguely amused. "No, Jack. Not the snowmobilers. Only a few deer. We've seen them out there before, haven't we?" It was true. When we first moved to the house, a small herd of deer liked to meander up the south side of the creek from across the road to the west; one looked like a fawn of six months or so—a spindly, cute, and skittish little creature. "And sometimes," Erika finished, "they can look pretty spooky, huh?"

"Sure," I said. It was true, too—if the deer were at the fringes of the glare of the spotlamp, as they often were, their coats reflected the light unevenly, and made them look tall, white, and quick-moving.

"Want a granola bar?" Erika nodded at the dining room table. I looked; she had half a granola bar on a blue saucer there, and an empty glass—it had obviously had milk in it.

"Is that why you got up, Erika? Because you were hungry?"

She nodded. "Uh-huh. Want some?"

"No. Thanks," I said.

"Oh?" She paused briefly; a sensuous grin started on her lips. "What *do* you want?"

"What do you think I want?"

"I think I want you," she said. "I think we want each other." It was a phrase we used to use quite a lot. "And I think that being spooked makes me horny, Jack."

She rarely used the word *horny*, and I liked it when she did. I whispered, "I didn't know that. That's nice to know."

She pushed against me—pelvis to pelvis. She said nothing.

"How horny does it make you, Erika?" I pushed back.

"Stop talking," she said.

"Sure," I said, and we both stopped talking for quite a while.

We got back to bed at around 3:00. I remember that she was shivering as we walked up the stairs and I asked her if she was cold. She turned and said, simply, "They *were* people, Jack." But by then it was too late, and I was too tired to care very much.

CHAPTER FOURTEEN

At the end of the first week in April a stocky, moon faced middle-aged man, wearing a yellow hunting jacket and carrying an over-and-under shotgun, came to the house and asked if he could use the phone. It was mid-morning, a little past eleven. He looked awfully agitated. He was even sweating a bit, although the temperatures that day hovered at just below fifty, so I asked him why he needed to use the phone.

He shook his head slightly. "No reason," he said. He smelled of gunpowder and cigars; his hunting boots were encased in mud.

"No reason?" I said.

He shook his head again, made a poor attempt at a *Nothing's wrong, really!* kind of smile. "There's been a little accident," he said, and inclined his head to the left. "Someone got shot."

"Oh, Jesus!" I murmured.

"So I need to use the phone"—another poor attempt at a smile—"I need to use the phone," he repeated, his voice quaking noticeably, "to call someone—"

I let him into the house, nodded at the phone on Erika's small desk in the library. "It's over there," I said.

"Thanks," he said, and went to it, picked it up, looked at it a moment, looked confusedly at me. "You think I should call the operator, and then she can call the sheriff, or you think I should call the hospital direct—"

"My God," I cut in, and went quickly over to him, took the phone. "Is the man dead?" I asked.

Another look of confusion. "What man?" he said.

"The man you *shot*, of course."

"I didn't shoot a man. I shot a woman."

"A woman? What woman?"

He shook his head. "I don't know. Some woman. I think she's dead."

"Where is she?"

He pointed toward the road in front of the house. "Across the road. In a gully." He grinned stupidly. "I thought she was a woodchuck. I shot her because I thought she was a woodchuck. What's your name?"

I put the phone down, put my hand on the barrel of the man's shotgun. "Leave that here, okay?" I said soothingly. "Leave that here, and show me where the woman is."

It had rained heavily the night before, reducing the last snow to sullen grayish patches at the bases of trees and around the garage and house. Much of the rest of the landscape was dark green, wet, and mashed flat from the weight of the snow.

At the crest of the mountain across the road the trees were white with ice. Now and again, the sun peeked out from behind a mantle of low, gray clouds, and its light danced crazily through the ice.

The hunter nodded. "That's real pretty, don't you think?"

We were halfway to the road then, halfway down the long, muddy slope of the driveway. I could see his footprints coming up it. "Where is the woman you shot?" I asked.

He pointed obliquely to the right, where the path leading up to Martin's house started. "She's over there, Mr. Harris."

"How'd you know my name?" I said.

He nodded at my mailbox. "Easy enough," he said.

I got my foot stuck in mud at the edge of the driveway. I tugged hard to free it, but without luck. I leaned over, pulled with both hands—which only made the suction stronger. The hunter didn't appear to notice this, and was at the road before he seemed to realize I was no longer walking with him. He looked around at me, grinned, lumbered back, shook his head slowly.

I said, "This is stupid."

"Suckin' you right up, ain't it, Mr. Harris?"

"This is incredibly stupid." I found it very difficult to believe that I couldn't get my foot out of the mud.

"You got to *ease* it out," he said.

"For God's sake, I've tried *easing* it out."

"No, you ain't. Just relax."

I tried to relax.

He said, "*Relax*, Mr. Harris!"

I relaxed.

"Let the mud do what it wants to do, Mr. Harris. It'll relax, too—you wait and see."

I said nothing. I didn't like the idea that I was receiving Good Country Wisdom from a near-idiot who'd shot a woman because he'd mistaken her for a woodchuck.

After a minute the mud did relax, and I slowly pulled my foot from it. I asked him again, "Where's the woman you shot?"

"Across the road," he answered. "In the gully." He started down the driveway again. I followed.

We found no woman. We found a spot where the outline in the wet grass was distinctly human, and the hunter said, pointing at it, "She was right here, on her stomach, Mr. Harris." There was no particular emphasis in his voice. "And her back was a real mess, 'cuz that's where I shot her. And she was wearing a dress. She was. She was wearing a long white dress. And her hair was real dark, down past the middle of her back. I cut some of it off with the shotgun pellets,''—this seemed to bother him a little; he sighed, hesitated, then went on—''and some of it was pushed into her back, where the wound was, you know, and she had her face into the ground, straight into it. You think of dead people, Mr. Harris, and you think their faces are turned this way or that, don'tcha? Sure. Hers wasn't. It was flat into the ground. And her arms were straight out and they were curved just a tad, like she was gonna hug someone. I think her name was Elizabeth. I seen her before. In Cohocton. I think I seen her at the tree-sitting festival. You go to that? Neat, huh? And I think some guy called her Elizabeth. Course I could be all wrong. I could be wrong about the whole thing, I guess. Maybe she wasn't dead, but, Gawd, she did have a awful big hole in her back—''

I broke in, finally. ''We have to call the police.''

He looked confusedly at me. ''What police?''

''The Cohocton Police.''

''We ain't got no police, Mr. Harris. We got a deputy sheriff and his name is Larry Whipple.''

''Shit,'' I whispered. I leaned over, fingered the area where the woman's body had been. ''There's no blood,'' I said.

The hunter said, ''Well, there wouldn't be, would there, 'cuz she was lying on her stomach, you know—''

''Don't be an idiot. Of course there'd be blood. I'd

smell it.'' The sun came out then, and its light hid the outline of the woman's body.

The hunter said, "You'd *smell* the blood?" I glanced around at him; a small, amused smile was on his face. "Wouldja now, Mr. Harris?" he added.

I shook my head, straightened. "I don't know. Maybe." Then I saw Martin's house, the house at the middle of the mountain that the snowmobilers had been going to several weeks earlier. I nodded at it. "Do you see that house?" I said.

The hunter looked. "Yeah I see it."

"And would you say that this"—I nodded at the ground—"is the property of the people who own that house?"

"Maybe."

"Then why didn't you go up there and talk to them? Why'd you come to me?"

He smiled again, a flat, long-suffering kind of smile. "Because *they're* crazy, Mr. Harris."

Larry Whipple offered his hand. I took it and let go of it almost immediately. "How you doing today, Mr. Harris?" he said. "John here tells me you've got some trouble again."

I shook my head. We were in the library; I noticed that John's muddy footprints were tracked across the Oriental rug, and I decided I'd try and vacuum it before Erika got home. John's shotgun was standing up in a far corner, near Erika's desk. "No, I haven't got any trouble at all," I said. "John's got the trouble." I went over to the shotgun, picked it up, held it horizontally in front of my belly. "Apparently, he's shot someone."

"Has he?" Whipple said, and turned to John, who was standing very quietly near the front door. He and Whipple had had a conference of sorts before coming into the house. "Who'd you shoot this time, John?" he said.

"He's shot other people?" I asked incredulously.

Whipple chuckled. He was dressed in the same clothes he was dressed in the first time I saw him—an orange hunting jacket, red flannel shirt, overalls, hiking boots—but this time he had a pistol strapped to his waist. "No, Mr. Harris, John's never shot a soul." He touched his temple. "John's not all there. John *wants* to shoot someone, you understand, but he doesn't know how to load his shotgun." He held his hand out to me. I gave him John's shotgun. He broke it open at the breach and held it up for me to see. "Empty," he said. "It's always empty." He closed the shotgun and gave it to John, who took it gladly and said, "Thanks, Larry. I was just having some fun, Larry," and the two of them excused themselves, went to Larry's car—a battered, decade-old Impala—and drove off.

A couple of minutes later I was back at the spot John had taken me to, and trying hard to find the outline of the woman's body in the matted grass. But the sun was out and I saw little. I looked about. The gully was shallow enough that my head stuck above its upper edges. Beyond it, to the east was the road, and three hundred feet east of that, our house. To the west the land lay flat for a good two or three hundred feet—there were fields of quack grass, an occasional cattail, some wild grape—and then angled very sharply upwards to the high hill where Martin's house was. For the first time, I could see this house very clearly. It was quite large, made of cedar logs, and had apparently been built on what appeared to be a small man-made plateau. The path leading to it was visible where it met the house; pine trees obscured the rest of it.

Smoke was drifting lazily up out of one of the house's two chimneys—at opposite ends of the severely sloping red-tiled roof—and I imagined that I could hear rock music playing, though very faintly.

I heard, from behind me, "We're not as crazy as they are, Mr. Harris." I turned quickly, surprised. Martin was standing just at the road's edge, with his hands in the pockets of his denim jacket.

I blurted, "A woman was shot here today."

"Uh-huh," the man said, and grinned knowledgeably. "Did John tell you that?"

"Yes."

"John's not very bright, Mr. Harris."

"So I was told."

"John has been known to lie on occasion."

"I'm not sure he was lying, Mr. Martin."

"And you may be right." Another smile. "How's your wife doing these days, Mr. Harris?"

I shook my head. "What has any of this to do with Erika?"

"That's her name? Erika?"

"Yes."

"That's a beautiful name. And this has quite a lot to do with her. I'm sorry." A pause. He went on, "Do you love her, Mr. Harris?"

"What kind of question is that?"

"Yes," he cut in, "naturally, you love her. And since you love her, you want to . . . hold on to her. Isn't that true?"

"I don't understand you, Mr. Martin."

"Just Martin. And of course you don't understand me." He looked down at his feet, stooped over, scooped up a handful of snow. He held it out on his open hand. "Try, Mr. Harris, to hold onto this." He let the snow drop. "It's the same sort of thing." He turned, and walked quickly north on the road, toward the path to his house. I called to him repeatedly— "Where are you going? This is important. Hey, come back here!"—but he ignored me.

When we'd been married not quite two years, Erika and I went to the funeral of my Aunt Lillian. Aunt Lillian had been in her late sixties and for the last two decades of her life had been incapacitated by one major illness after another—diabetes, encephalitis, acute arthritis. It was cancer that killed her.

She was a very cheerful, bright woman, an optimist to her last day, when, apparently knowing that the cancer had caught up with her, she looked at my mother, who was her younger sister, and said, smiling, "No more illness. Just the fresh air."

I repeated this story to Erika when we were driving to the funeral. She appeared to have little reaction beyond a small sigh and a nod of the head. But when we got to the funeral, she went ahead of me to the casket, touched it, and whispered, "Yes. You're right."

I probably should have told Erika about John and Larry Whipple and Martin, but I never did. It's the same old story. I was trying to protect her, although I knew the chances were good that she'd be able to handle the thing I was hiding from her. But I did hide it from her. I took her to a movie in Canandaigua—thirty miles east of Cohocton—a movie which we both hated, then out for a snack at a place called The Eatery, which had stark pretensions to elegance, and we hated that, too, and when we got home, at half past twelve, we found that the house had been vandalized.

CHAPTER FIFTEEN

I didn't call Larry Whipple. I called the Dansville substation of the New York State Police and was told that an investigator would be sent over immediately. Erika and I tallied up the damage while we waited. We found that there was damage in each room; some of it was minor—graffiti on the bedroom wall read GREETINGS! in big, red block letters above the bed— and some of it was vicious; in the laundry room, a floor lamp had been taken apart and the pole used to put a dozen deep, wide gouges in all four walls. In the library, Erika's cherry desk had been smashed with an axe taken from the garage—the axe was left leaning in the corner where I'd put John's shotgun—and in the kitchen, the electric stove had been crudely rigged to the sink, so that someone turning on the stove and then going to use the faucets would get a hell of a shock. Or that was apparently the intention. It was so very crudely done that it would never have worked.

Erika and I wandered about in a kind of daze from room to room, taking in the damage. A grandfather's clock I'd spent nearly a month building from a kit had had its guts torn out, though the cabinet was left untouched. Graffiti—in the same red block letters that were used in the bedroom—were everywhere; some of the graffiti read simply, HI! or WE'RE HERE! or, in the downstairs powder room, WE'RE HERE NOW! (to which I responded at a whisper, "Yes, I can see that!"), and in the dining room, the word CEILING had been written, predictably, on the ceiling. "He's a comedian," I said to Erika. She said nothing.

The investigator from the Dansville State Police substation didn't arrive until a little past 1:30. He was a short, slightly built black man with a head full of tight curls, and he was wearing a black suit and vest. He looked very much like he'd just come from a wedding. His name was Mansfield Barnes, and the first thing he said to us was, "Do you folks have any pets?"

Erika said, "We have a cat. Well, we *had* two cats, one ran away—"

"And do you know where the remaining cat is?" Barnes interrupted.

"No," I said.

"Find the cat, please," Barnes said.

"Sure," I said, and went looking for Orphan. I looked in the living room first, and then in the library, and then behind the buffet in the dining room, which had gone untouched by the vandalism. I called for him: "Orphan, come here, Orphan!" and kept it up as I walked into the kitchen, Erika and Barnes following. I heard Erika say, behind him, "How is the cat important?"

"We've had some problems with vandalism in Dansville," Barnes explained, "and I'm afraid that household pets have been the chief target—"

I cut in, "No. There he is." Orphan was in the kitchen, behind the table, eating.

Erika asked, "Jack, what's he eating?"

I moved closer to the cat. It had one paw on the belly of a dead raccoon. The raccoon's head was tilted at right angles to its body, and its body moved in rhythm with the cat's long, slow licking movements. As the cat licked, it purred in great contentment.

"My God," I said, "they fed the cat."

And Mansfield Barnes said, "This is not what's been happening in Dansville at all, not at all."

I took the raccoon far into the woods behind the house and buried it as deep as I could—which, because the ground was still hard, wasn't very deep at all. One of its black feet stuck up above the grave.

Then, with the aid of a flashlight, I made my way back to the house.

I went in through the kitchen door, called, "Erika, where are you?" I got no answer and went into the dining room, where I called for her again. She'd begun to put the house in order. The piano, which had been tilted on end, had been righted—with Mansfield Barnes's help, I supposed—and the pine dining table—the word HELLO had been scratched into the middle of it in the same big block letters—had a clean white tablecloth over it.

"Erika?" I called, and when I still got no answer I called again, louder, "Erika, where the hell are you?"

Mansfield Barnes called from upstairs, "Here, Mr. Harris. In the bedroom. In the master bedroom. Could you please come up?"

I went quickly up the stairs, looked into the master bedroom, saw no one. "Where are you?" I called.

"In the closet, Jack," Erika called back.

I went to the closet—it was a huge walk-in closet with a high ceiling and an entire wall's worth of built-in drawers; I'd joked with Erika once that it would make a nifty guest bedroom for some of our in-laws. Mansfield Barnes and Erika were at the center of it, the bare, wall-mounted light fixture switched on, their gaze on the ceiling overhead. I looked up, too. Written in big, red block letters there were the words AND WE'RE STILL HERE!

"Real comedians," I said, and Mansfield Barnes said simply: "Uh-huh, they're everywhere."

*   *   *

"We've got to shellac the entire ceiling, don't we, Jack?" Erika said much later, in bed. The beginnings of daylight were visible through the windows. The curtains had been torn down by the vandals and now lay in a heap on the bedroom floor.

"I don't know if it's shellac we have to use, Erika. That tile"—the ceilings throughout the house had been done in porous, beige acoustical tile—"will soak up paint like a sponge, I know. But I'm not sure that shellac would do the trick because then we'd have the problem of painting over the shellac, and I've done that and you get into all kinds of moisture problems—"

"You could ask at the hardware store, Jack. I'm sure there's some sort of sealant you can buy." Her words were slow, very measured, but I could hear tension in them, and something else, too—resolve, I realized, and I thought, incorrectly, that it was a resolve to put the house in order as quickly as possible. She continued, "We certainly can't leave it the way it is."

"It'd be unique," I said.

"Yeah," she said, "unique." She paused briefly, continued, "Why'd they write that stuff all over the house, Jack?"

"Just your basic creative vandal, I suppose. He knew what would scare us."

"He scared the hell out of me."

"He scared me, too, Erika."

A minute's silence, then: "Where'd you bury that raccoon, Jack?"

"Out back," I answered. "Way out back. And deep. Good and deep."

"Uh-huh." She was whispering now, low and tight. "Don't lie to me, Jack. I don't like it. The ground's still hard, so how deep could you have buried it?"

"Deep enough."

"I hope so. I don't want to trip over it in the spring; that wouldn't make my day."

"You won't."

She said nothing.

I said, "God, I'm sorry this happened, Erika."

Still nothing.

"You going to sleep?"

"No."

"Oh. You can't sleep, huh?"

"Eventually I will." A pause. "Jack?" She sounded troubled.

"Yes?"

"Is something wrong?"

I chuckled a small, false chuckle. "Is something wrong?!" I said sarcastically. "Here, her house gets vandalized, her belongings destroyed—"

"It doesn't matter, Jack. Really, it doesn't matter at all. I just wanted you to know something. I wanted to tell you that what I've learned about love, what I know about love, Jack . . ." She seemed tongue-tied. "I wanted you to know that I love you. Whatever you think that means, whatever you think love means, it's what I mean."

I said nothing. She sounded intensely earnest, confused, a little sad.

She added, "We'll be here, at this house, Jack— you and I will be at this house for a good long time. I know that."

"Yes," I said. "I know that, too, Erika. That's what I want."

"I feel like I'm drifting, Jack."

"Drifting?" I knew that she'd used the word before when she was talking about herself, but I couldn't remember in what context.

"I feel . . . apart—" She sounded very confused now.

"Erika, my God, what's wrong?"

"There's nothing wrong." She sounded convinced of that. I wished that the light was on so I could read her face. "Could you do me a favor, Jack?"

"Sure." I put my hand on the top of hers, got no reaction. "Name it."

"Fix the curtains."

"You mean right now?"

"Yes. If you don't mind. You can jerry-rig them. I'll help you." She was pleading with me. "We can stick the rods up and throw the curtains over them. We can use blankets, if that's easier. It's too light in here." It wasn't light at all. "It's too close to morning, Jack. I won't be able to sleep." She still was pleading. "I need the dark. I'm sorry. I need the dark."

"Sure, Erika." I got out of the bed and, alone, spent the next half hour putting the curtains up. When I got back into bed, she was asleep. I leaned over and kissed her cheek. "I love you, too," I said. "I love you a lot," and from what I could see of her face, I supposed that she smiled as she slept, which made me feel better than I'd felt in a long time.

I woke several hours later. I heard talking in the house. I heard talking from the room below, which is the library, from the guest room, from the big open room, from the house itself, as if the walls were talking.

I could make out no words. I could hear only the *sense* of the words, a sense of quiet urgency, the way a doctor speaks to a woman giving birth.

I did not wake Erika to hear it. It lasted only a few seconds.

CHAPTER SIXTEEN

Our memories do sustain us. They give the present a backdrop, scenery, substance; they tell us who we are and what we're becoming, and if what we're becoming is worth anything at all.

Our memories sing to us, too. And caress us. And chill us, hurt us, make us numb, so that we sit for hours quietly, unmoving and unchanging because that will put time off, and the moments will not happen.

I used to do that quite a lot at the house when Erika wasn't there. I used to sit in a big wing-backed chair in the living room and listen to the noises that the house made, and I used to say to myself that it would never change, that the house would stand forever, that Erika and I would live forever in it, because that's what *was* and how could it possibly change if I kept watching it?

It's what I was doing the day after the vandalism happened. Erika had taken off for the afternoon. We'd awakened late and she'd had a cup of coffee and said simply, "I've got to get out of here for a couple hours, Jack." Then she got into her blue Volvo and was gone.

I sat in the wing-backed chair and I thought, in so many words, *Something's happening to her. She's changing!* I wondered if it was life at the house that was doing it or if, perhaps, her attitude toward me was changing; I dearly hoped not.

In the room around me, things were much as we'd found them the night before. The big oak grandfather's clock I'd labored on so long and lovingly stood with its waist door open and the chain and weights, the pendulum, chimes and chime board scattered on the floor. In front of me, the gray art-deco couch that Erika and I had bought four years earlier, our first major purchase, lay on its back, its underside torn apart. Above the fireplace—a bare wall that lots of people had been after us to "put something on"— still more graffiti asked, in the same red block letters, WHERE DO THE CHILDREN PLAY? It was, I remembered, a line from a Cat Stevens song.

In the fireplace itself, toward the front of it, there

were what looked like partial footprints in the ashes.

"You'll get your locks changed, of course," Mansfield Barnes had said. "You'll get dead bolts."

And I answered, nodding at the footprints, "Maybe that wouldn't do any good, Mr. Barnes. Maybe these people came down the chimney."

To which Barnes, with great stoicism, replied, "That wouldn't be possible, now would it?"

And I realized, as I sat in the wing-backed chair, that I'd begun to miss Erika. Not for that moment, not because she'd gone off in her blue Volvo. But that I'd begun missing the Erika who slept with the night-light on, the Erika who got a big kick out of Kliban cats, the Erika who gave me arguments about politics—we had certain basic disagreements in that area—and who occasionally had fun with my tastes in art and movies—I liked Andrew Wyeth; she thought he was starkly commercial; I enjoyed reruns of old Steve Martin movies; she thought he was simply a buffoon.

And I missed the Erika who often made a game out of lovemaking, who played the role of a vamp, or a prostitute, or a "sweet young thing"—as she said—and carried the act out to the end, grinning and chuckling through her passion now and again. (I remembered that several months earlier, for my birthday, she'd given me an official-looking hardcover book titled *An Analysis of Keynesian Economic Theory and its Bilateral Effects on Third World Industrial Growth.*

("Very nice, Erika," I said, and she pointed at the bottom of the cover. There were some words in tiny gray print, so they were nearly invisible on the light blue background—*How to Have Multiple Orgasms*.

("Oh," I said, grinning, and flipped through the pages. They were blank, except at the center, where a stylized Viking woman proclaimed, spear in hand, "Do it over and over and over again!")

Sex was very important to her, but she always had great fun with it, and I thought that was healthy. But, in the last month, that had changed. Now she made love with an overwhelming and passionate intensity that scared me at times because she did it as if her life depended on it. And she sometimes said, when it was done, "Thank you, Jack." To which I usually replied, for lack of anything better to say, "You're welcome, Erika. Gee, let's do it again sometime."

I drove to Granada that afternoon. I went there because I supposed that I'd find Sarah Talpey there. I didn't.

I found Granada inhabited.

I found people mowing lawns, washing cars, walking dogs, trimming hedges, pushing baby carriages.

And as I drove through Granada, heads turned, I got quizzical looks, a few smiles, I got ignored, someone yelled, "Hi."

But there were no lawns to mow in Granada, and no lawnmowers, or baby carriages, no hedges to trim, or hedge trimmers, or cars to wash.

Only people pretending to do the things that people who live in places like Granada do.

And it was clear that they believed the things they were doing because they did them with such earnest intensity. As if they'd been doing those things all their lives.

They were dressed for spring, in light jackets and double-knit slacks, in gardener's pants, in wide-brimmed hats, in Izod shirts, and peasant dresses.

I stopped. I rolled the window down a crack.

"Hi," someone said again.

"Hi," someone else said.

"Hi," said a man nearby who was going through the motions of washing a car. "Come over later, have a beer."

And I saw a dark-haired, dark-skinned woman in a beige blouse stick her head out of a first-floor window. "Where are the children playing?" she called. Some faces turned toward her. There were some desultory shrugs; someone—the man close to me, I think—said with obvious disinterest, "I don't know," as if she were trying to involve him in a game of trivia and he didn't want to go along with it.

And then he turned toward me. His right hand—the hand that would have been holding the garden hose—moved further to the right, so he wouldn't splash me. But I had my foot off the brake then, and I heard nothing of what he had to say; only this: "And you—"

And I was gone.

*   *   *

I found Sarah on Clement Road. She was carrying her sleeping bag under one arm, what looked like an attaché case under the other, and when I stopped beside her and rolled the window down—"Sarah?" I said—she didn't acknowledge me. She kept walking. Her head was lowered slightly; she had that little frown on her mouth. I moved the car forward thirty feet or so, stopped, jumped out, and called back to her, "Sarah? Where are you going?"

She looked up at last. Her frown was replaced briefly by a friendly, flat, and tired smile. "Oh. Jack, isn't it?" she said. "Good to see you. Have you been to Granada?"

"Yes," I said, and took the sleeping bag from her.

"They're back, Jack."

"Why don't you come to the car, Sarah?"

She stopped walking, glanced around toward Granada, then back at me. "I had to leave my truck there, Jack. I was beginning to like that truck. I don't often grow attached to machinery. I detest machinery. I own a typewriter, but I never use it. Someone tried once to explain to me how computers work, and I didn't understand a word of it. But I did like that truck, Jack."

"Get in the car, Sarah, please."

"I'll go back for it. When they're gone. I don't think they're going to stay. I think they'll be out of there in a day or so." She looked confusedly at me. "How do you judge these things, Jack? How do you judge something that you've never before experienced? I don't know *why* they're there. I woke up this morning, and there they were. All around me. Like flies.''

"Come to the car, Sarah." I took her arm, coaxed her toward the car.

"I thought they were kind of . . . entertaining, at first, Jack. Really. Entertaining. As if they were putting on a show for me. They weren't, of course. They believed what they were doing. I knew that. I could *see* that.''

I continued coaxing her to the car. I opened the Toyota's passenger door, tossed the sleeping bag onto the backseat. "Get in, Sarah. Buckle up.''

She got in. She buckled up.

I went around to the other side, got in, pulled away from the shoulder. I felt her touch my hand.

"You know,'' she said, and her tone was suddenly one of excitement, "we really should go back there. It's a marvelous anthropological opportunity. They've *returned*, Jack." She paused. "Of course, they're awfully damned spooky. And you can't really talk to them. I tried it. I said to one of the women, 'Why are you doing that?' She was in the house I was using, Jack. She was vacuuming the floor. She had all the motions right—my God, she even ran over the cord a couple of times and cursed at it. But there was no cord. And there was no vacuum cleaner. And she was such a *beautiful* woman. A real knockout. 'Because the floor's dirty,' she said. I asked her who she was. 'I don't know,' she said.''

I tromped on the accelerator then, because I'd

glanced in the rearview mirror and had seen a group
of five or six people coming our way.

Sarah continued. "And it occurred to me that they
were probably dangerous. I didn't realize at first *who*
they were. I mean, *who* they were"—out of the
corner of my eye I saw a wide, amused smile on her
face—"was really so improbable—impossible, actually—that it didn't occur to me. And it never occurred to me that they would come back to Granada
after twenty years. So of course I thought they were
just a bunch of crazies."

I glanced in the rearview mirror. The group of five
or six people there looked, incredibly, to be at the
same distance. I pushed harder on the accelerator,
got the Toyota up to sixty-five, then seventy. "Keep
talking, Sarah."

"I am talking, Jack. And please don't drive so
fast. It's incautious."

"We're being followed."

"Of course we are."

I glanced quickly at her. She gave me a knowing
smile, touched my hand. "Jack, I'm afraid they have
certain . . . powers. So it really will do little good—"

The front right tire hit a deep pothole. I heard
myself curse, felt the steering wheel being wrenched
from my grip, realized that Sarah's hand was still on
mine, that she was still smiling at me as we went off
the road. The Toyota rolled once, and again. Finally,
it came to rest on its roof.

CHAPTER SEVENTEEN

"We've flipped over," Sarah said. She was strapped in; the shoulder harness was holding her in place.

I wasn't strapped in, and when the car had rolled, I'd hung onto the steering wheel and hoped for the best, though it had done little good. I realized, painfully, that my shoulder was probably broken.

"Sarah," I managed, "I'm hurt."

"Of course you are."

"I need help."

"We both do, Jack." Her tone had become deadly serious.

I tried to gauge the position I was in, tried to determine if I could push my door open. I wiggled the fingers of both hands, felt an odd tingling sensation in my right hand, then moved the hands themselves and my right arm. My left arm wouldn't move.

"You look like hell, Jack."

"I feel like hell."

"Are we going to stay in here, or what?"

"I think I have to. I'm in a little bit of pain, Sarah."

"I can't move you." A short pause. "I can move myself, but I can't move you." She fumbled with the seat belt. After a few moments she said, "There's a small problem, Jack. I can't get the seat belt to work."

"It's jammed?"

"No. My weight's on it." I heard the beginnings of anger in her voice. "My weight's on it, Jack, so I can't make it work. If I took my weight off it—if I took my damned weight off it—Christ, why do they make them like this?!—why would anyone make a goddamned seat belt that you can't get out of if you're upside down in it? Can you tell me that, Jack?" She was fumbling with the seat belt as she spoke. "Can you? I know this situation is just a little unusual, but why in the name of heaven couldn't someone somewhere have designed a seat belt that works under all situations and conditions?" I was beginning to find some perverse comfort in her tempered intellectual anger. "People are so damned enamored of their gadgets and their machinery and their mechanical toys, but they have never figured out how to make *some* things well." She continued fumbling. "Toilet seats, for instance. A marvel of anti-engineering. And women's shoes. Electric can openers. Ice cube trays. Christ—and seat belts!" She cursed under her breath; it was clear that she cursed rarely because, even in those circumstances, she didn't want me to hear her. Finally she said, "Got it!" and a moment later found herself sprawled on the roof of the car. She chuckled once or twice. Then a man's face appeared at her window and a little screech erupted from her.

The man said, "You got a problem here, don't-cha?!"

I groaned. And Sarah, after several moments to compose herself, said almost matter-of-factly, "Yes. We have a problem. Could you help us?"

We were taken to the Dansville Memorial Hospital. Sarah wasn't seriously injured, though she had sprained her neck slightly in the fall from the seat to the roof of the car. My shoulder was cracked, and the ring finger of my right hand smashed. I remember shaking my head and grinning when the doctor—a short, balding man named John Wilson who spoke in a high monotone—told me all that. "Jesus," I said, "it sure hurts like hell." I had already been put in a hospital bed.

"It's nothing that won't mend nicely in time, Mr. Harris," Wilson said, nodding and smiling his reassurance. "You're going to have to stay with us a few days, though I imagine you guessed as much."

"I did." I glanced about the tiny, beige-colored room. "Is there a phone handy?" I asked. "I'd like to call my wife."

Wilson said, predictably, "We've tried to do that already, Mr. Harris. One of the intake people is in charge of it." Another reassuring nod and smile. "I'll check to see if she's made any progress if you'd like."

"Yes." I tried for a friendly smile but it felt strange. "If you don't mind."

He nodded again and left the room. He came back less than a minute later, smiled, said, "They couldn't get hold of her, Mr. Harris. They've been trying, but, apparently, she hasn't been home. Does she work?"

"She isn't at work," I said, and realized that the tranquilizers were taking hold because I wasn't sure I'd said anything at all. "She isn't at work," I repeated.

"She isn't at work?" Wilson asked.

"No. She didn't go in today."

"I see. And you don't know where she is?"

I sighed. "This is getting a little silly, Dr. Wilson."

"Perhaps." A short pause. "Do you know how long you've been with us, Mr. Harris?"

"I think I was brought in an hour or so ago," I said. "A couple of hours ago."

He shook his head. "You were brought in yesterday afternoon. I'm sorry. It's the tranquilizers. Just the tranquilizers. You've been drifting in and out of consciousness—and coherence—since you got here.

And we've been trying to contact your wife since then."

"Are you sure you have the right number?"

"We got it from the telephone book."

"And how often have you tried calling her?"

"Quite often, Mr. Harris. You need some minor surgery, I'm afraid, and next of kin need to be consulted on such matters, not, of course, that we can't go ahead with it without their consent—"

"She should be at home, damnit!"

"She's not, Mr. Harris. At least she isn't answering the phone. You look upset. Don't be. These things are often simply a matter of coincidence. We call; she's not there. She comes home; we don't call." Another reassuring nod and smile. "And of course, there's the fact that she's worried about you, which I'm positive does quite a lot to modify her comings and goings. If need be, I know some people in your area, and I can have them check your house to make sure everything's all right."

"Of course everything's all right."

"Of course." A short pause. "I have other patients to tend to, Mr. Harris. Why don't you get some sleep? I'll let you know if we succeed in contacting your wife."

Erika drove off in her blue Volvo and was gone. That's the last I remembered of her. I remembered that the Volvo spat some gray exhaust fumes when she turned onto Hunt's Hollow Road and I said to myself that it might need a tune-up. I remember she put her hand to her hair, as if she were patting down some errant curl, when she accelerated to the south. I remember that I waved a little from the front window of the house, but she wasn't looking, so she didn't wave back. And when I took these memories out and looked at them, I got frustrated, and I got angry, because they weren't the kind of memories that parting should be made of. They were quick and purposeless, and they didn't mean anything.

CHAPTER EIGHTEEN

My brother Will went to the house three days after the accident. He said when I called that he could hear the tension in my voice, and although it was a long drive for him, he agreed at once to go to the house.

He came to my room at Dansville Memorial Hospital early on my fourth evening there. He was dressed in jeans, a white, long-sleeved shirt, a denim jacket, and he looked scruffy and tired. He shook my hand, backed away a few steps, said I looked awful, which I conceded, and then he added, ''I couldn't find her, Jack. Maybe she's left you or something."

I shook my head. "No, Will, she's finished doing that kind of thing . . ."

He cut in, "Your house is a mess."

"It was vandalized."

"You told me. I cleaned some of it up for you."

"Thanks."

"I fed your cat, too. She was awfully hungry, Jack. I thought you had two cats."

"We did. One ran off."

"Then I went looking for Erika. I hear you were with some other woman when the accident happened."

I sighed. "I was with a friend who happens to be a woman."

"Not that it matters," he said. "I mean, Erika's missing, and that's what matters, isn't it?" I started to answer. He hurried on, "I just can't help but think that she knew about this woman, Jack, and that she left you because of her; you certainly couldn't blame her if that's what she did."

"Let's not get off on tangents, Will—"

"I agree. This woman you were with is hardly the point; I agree." He glanced quickly about. "How long do you think they're going to keep you, Jack?"

"A couple more days. Will, we're going to have to stick to the subject here, and the subject is Erika."

"Sorry."

"Did she leave a note?"

"No. No note, Jack. Are you saying that she knew about this other woman?"

"For Christ's sake, there is no other woman. There

is only Erika; there has always been only Erika, and I'm worried as hell about her. I'm at the point where I'm going to go looking for her myself—''

"I called the police, Jack."

"You did *what*?"

He sighed, realized that he had overstepped his bounds, though it was hardly the first time. "I called the police. I was worried about her. I still am. You should be, too. They asked if she had a history, you know—a history of taking off unannounced. And she does, of course, which is what I told them. And they said to sit tight. That's what they said, Jack. 'Sit tight.' Stupid, huh?"

"Christ, Will, I wish you hadn't done that. I know she's coming back."

"So do I, Jack. Of course. We both know she's coming back."

My room at the Dansville Hospital had one window. It faced south and looked out on an abandoned farm. I knew the farm was abandoned because one of the orderlies told me it was: "This man and woman worked it for a few years, then they split. It happens all the time around here—the soil's not much good for nothin' but grapes."

I got used to seeing people there—around the farm— during the seven days I spent in the hospital. It was a quarter mile from the hospital, but at the top of a gradual slope, bare of trees. From that distance, the farmhouse looked sturdy and freshly painted—white— especially when the sun was shining on it, although the same orderly told me, "It's a fuckin' *dis*grace. Christ, they oughta burn the damn thing to the ground."

I got into the habit of watching people come and go from that farmhouse. Always the same people: a man in green overalls, a woman in a long blue coat, a woman in white, a man in a dark suit, a woman in a green dress and beige jacket who always seemed to lag behind the others. They had a routine. They arrived at the farmhouse at around 9:00 in the morning and milled about (several of them looked my way a couple of times). Then the man in green overalls wandered off, away from the house; the woman in the long blue coat wandered after him several minutes later, and the others went into the house, though briefly. When they came out, they moved off in the same direction as the first two.

The orderly saw this once. He watched the man in green overalls move down the slope, watched the woman follow minutes later, watched as the others went into the house, left it, went in the same direction as the first two. "Who's those assholes?" he said to himself.

I said, "They've been doing that for a week now."

"What the fuck for?" he asked.

"I don't know. Do they need a reason?"

He smiled at this, as if he'd caught on that I was being philosophical with him and he wasn't going to have any part of it. "People got to have *reasons* for what they do, you know."

* * *

Most of my time at the hospital was spent trying, through Will, to find Erika. He agreed to check on the house as often as possible. This turned out to be a daily thing because he got a motel room in North Cohocton for the length of my hospital stay. I asked him why he didn't simply stay at the house.

"Because it spooks the hell out of me, Jack," he answered, which was a phrase I never expected to hear from him.

"What do you mean, it spooks the hell out of you?"

He shook his head. "I don't know. Christ, Jack, I don't know." A brief pause. "It *talks*; that's what I mean. The damn house talks."

And I said nothing.

CHAPTER NINETEEN

When I was discharged from the hospital, I talked Will into giving me a ride back to the house. He was quiet for most of the thirty-minute drive, which was unlike him. He was dressed in a dark blue pin-striped suit and sat very erect in the driver's seat, eyes straight ahead, as if he wanted me to be quiet, too.

He broke his silence when we were halfway back to the house. "Do cars scare you now, Jack?"

"No," I said. "Should they?"

He shrugged. "No. I suppose not. It was just a thought."

We turned onto Hunt's Hollow Road, three miles from the house. He said, "I cleaned things up for you. I got rid of the graffiti. I put the parts to your clock in the spare room. In a box. I think you'll be able to fix that clock. It's a nice clock; you *should* try to fix it. There wasn't much I could do with Erika's desk. I left it for you to take care of. I suppose you'll throw it out, right? Seems a shame."

"What's on your mind, Will?" I cut in. It had always been very clear to me when something was bothering him. "Is it Erika?"

A group of people were walking on the shoulder. He slowed the car, went halfway into the left-hand lane to avoid them.

He went back into the right lane, glanced in the rearview mirror. "I've always liked Erika. I guess you know that."

"I know that. I like her, too."

"But you're giving up, right?"

"No." I said, and I meant it. "I'm not giving up."

He slowed the car again. A young woman in a white dress had appeared from thickets that crowded the shoulder here and was crossing the road just a hundred feet or so ahead of us. "Who the hell is that?" I said.

"I don't know," Will said matter-of-factly. She finished crossing the road and disappeared into the thickets on the other side. Will speeded up. "I think you are," he said.

"Are what?"

"Giving up on Erika."

"The shit I am. Jesus, Will, you've always had the wrong fucking idea of me, haven't you?"

"There's no need to get upset, Jack. I know we have different . . . outlooks—" Again he slowed the car, this time for two people, a man and a woman, who were walking well into our lane. He went into the left lane, glanced again in the rearview mirror, muttered "Jesus!" and then turned the car into my driveway, stomped on the accelerator—also unlike him—so the rear tires spit gravel and mud onto Hunt's Hollow Road. The car shot forward. He brought it to an abrupt halt in front of the house, behind the bare privet hedges, and scared the hell out of Orphan, who'd been sleeping near them.

I asked angrily, "What was *that* all about?"

"Sorry," he said. "Let's go inside, Jack, okay? We'll talk there. I really don't like staying out here too long."

"Why the hell not?"

He gave me a flat, sardonic grin. "You'll see," he said.

He'd found some snapshots of Erika, had bought frames for them, and had set them up on the piano in the dining room. Some of the photographs were a few years old and showed Erika with short hair and various scarves tied around her neck. I used to kid her that this was her "preppy period." The other photographs were quite recent. One showed her standing in front of the house, beneath the big window, with her hands behind her back and a broad, apparently pleased smile on her face. I remembered that she was smiling like that only because I'd been tickling her.

I couldn't help but see these newly framed and newly exhibited photographs as a kind of shrine to Erika, and it made me angry. I began taking them off the piano as soon as I saw them.

"Please leave them there, Jack," Will said half angrily, half in hurt.

"For Christ's sake, Will! You said that *I* was giving up—"

"I thought you'd be pleased." His tone had changed; now it was apologetic. "I thought you'd like them."

My left arm was still in a cast, and I couldn't carry all the photographs in my right hand. I nodded at the extras. "Bring those, would you, please?" I asked Will.

"Sure," he said.

We took them into the music room and put them in a chest of drawers that Erika stored sheet music in.

"She's coming back, Will," I said. "God, I believe that. I really do believe that." We went back to the dining room.

"I know she's coming back," Will said, but he sounded unconvinced and unconvincing. He shook his head quickly. "Jack?" He looked away, toward the window that faced the side yard. "You probably shouldn't stay here," he went on. "It's probably not wise for you to stay here."

"Why the hell not?"

"Because there are . . . people—"

I took the last photograph of Erika down from the piano. It showed her feeding a black, lop-eared goat at a place called Wildwood Farms, a couple of miles away. I looked at the snapshot a moment, remembered that it was I who had framed it and put it on the piano, so I put it back. "You mean those people we saw on the road, Will?" I asked. "Who are they?" I tried to sound unconcerned. In the hospital I had heard a little, from Will, about "strangers around the house," but most of the times that he'd telephoned or had come in to see me, I'd been coming out of or going into the effects of painkillers or tranquilizers and most of what he'd told me had gone all but unheard. "Are they supposed to be dangerous?"

"No one knows," Will said.

"No one knows? That's a pretty odd thing to say, isn't it, Will?" I sat on the piano bench; the ride from the hospital had tired me out. "Have they hurt anyone, threatened anyone? What's the big deal?"

Will pulled a dining room chair out, sat down noisily, and folded his hands on top of the table. "No," he said. "They're just . . . there. And as long as they don't trespass, there's not much that can be done about them." He paused. "They're just there, Jack." It seemed to confuse him.

"Well, my God, Will," I said, "this is stupid! What are they doing? Where do they stay? I mean, they must stay *some*place."

"I guess they do," Will said. He unfolded his

hands, sat back and folded his arms over his stomach.
"Of course they do. I'm sure there are lots of places
they can stay. And what's-his-name, Whipple, has
been watching them. He's even arrested a few of
them for trespassing, but he's let them go because no
one wants to press charges." He looked earnestly at
me, his hands still folded across his belly. "Jack,
they're everywhere. I mean, they're on the main
roads; they're on the dirt roads; they're out in the
fields—on posted land, of course. But I guess Whipple and his hired cretins can't be everywhere. And
I've seen them around this house, too."

"Yes," I said. "So have I." He didn't seem to
hear me.

"And I can't help but think, Jack, that they had
something to do with Erika's . . ." He faltered.

"That they had something to do with her disappearance," I coaxed.

"Okay," he said. "That's okay. I'll accept that."
He stopped, shook his head again. "This is all very
strange, Jack. This is very, very spooky. I loved
Erika; I *love* Erika—"

"Christ, don't you think I realize that, Will? I love
her, too. I've been married to her for six years. We
bought this house together, and by God, we're going
to live in it—" And then I stopped because I saw a
man standing at the window. "Good Lord," I
whispered. I got up quickly from the piano bench,
ran to the side door, pushed the screen door open,
went outside and looked to the right. The man
was walking slowly off, toward the front of the

house. I yelled to him to stop. He turned his head slightly. "Damn you!" I yelled after him, and stepped off the porch. A light rain had started. "Get off my property!" I yelled, and felt immediately foolish for it, as if the man were merely a salesman or a Jehovah's Witness and I was being incredibly rude to him.

I caught up with him near Will's car and put my hand on his shoulder to pull him around. He turned voluntarily. He was tall, dark, had magnificent blue eyes. And when he turned he gave me a broad, disarming smile. He was dressed casually, in brown corduroy pants, faded blue shirt, a worn-out brown tweed jacket. He said, "I'm sorry. I lost my way." I realized from his tone that it was the truth.

"You certainly did," I said, but my anger had been tempered by his honesty and by his smile. "What were you looking for?"

"I don't know," he said.

"What do you mean, you 'don't know'?"

He shook his head, was clearly confused. "I was born here," he announced.

"Do you mean at this house?"

He looked at the house for a moment. His confusion seemed to lessen and his smile broadened, as if in recognition. "I don't think so," he said. "I'm not sure." He looked quizzically at me. "Do you know me? Have you seen me before?"

"No," I answered.

"Oh." He seemed to think about that. Then he asked, "And you don't know my name?"

"Of course I don't know your name."

"But I was *born* here!" He had suddenly become agitated. He swept his arm wide to indicate the landscape behind me. "I remember this."

"I'm going to have to ask you please to get off my property; I'm sorry—"

He grabbed my wrists, squeezed hard, pulled me closer angrily. "I *remember* this!" he repeated. He was incredibly strong. "I know that my *mother* is here!" And he let me go.

I stepped away from him, felt myself shaking. "Please," I managed.

"I am *human*!" he screeched. "My mother is here!"

I took a deep breath, tried to think of something to say, felt doubly frightened. At last I said, "I'm going to have to ask you to stay off my property. Otherwise I'll be forced to phone the police."

His wide, disarming smile reappeared. "I'm human," he whispered. Then he turned, walked quickly around Will's Mercedes, passed between it and the privet hedge—he let his fingers trace a crooked line in the beaded moisture on the Mercedes—then strolled down the long, muddy driveway and crossed the road.

I heard Will come up behind me. I turned my head.

"Jesus," Will said, "you can't *talk* to them, Jack. I've tried *talking* to them."

We watched as the man descended into the gully across the road, then appear moments later on the other side of it. He was moving very quickly now, at a fast and consummately graceful walk rather than a run.

"I've talked to that one before," Will went on. "I've *tried* to talk to him, anyway. All I could get from him was that his name is Seth and that he came here from Manhattan. I asked him where he's staying. He wouldn't tell me. I asked him what he was doing here—on your land—and he wouldn't tell me that, either. So I called Whipple about him, and Whipple came down and looked for him (at least he *said* he looked for him), but he couldn't find him."

I started for the house. Will fell in beside me. He cupped his hand on my left elbow. "Are you okay, Jack? You looked tired."

"Of course I'm tired." The rain was steady and soft now, the air frigid. "I'm cold, too, and I'm wet."

"I'll stay here with you for a few days, Jack."

"That's not necessary." I reached to open the screen door, saw that my hand was shaking.

Will reached quickly around me. "I'll get that," he said, and opened the door. I glanced at him; he was smiling foolishly. "You need me around here," he said. He pushed the kitchen door open.

I went inside.

"You really do need me around, Jack." He followed me to the dining room table. We sat. "Jack?" he said, and I heard something tense in his voice.

"Yes?"

He shook his head, grinned foolishly again, glanced out the window behind me. "I don't know how to say this.'' He looked earnestly at me. "I don't know how to say it without sounding . . . melodramatic, but I *feel* that Erika is here. I feel that she's here. In this house.''

CHAPTER TWENTY

I told him to get out. He apologized several times, and at length, added, "I'm probably just hitching myself to a wish-fulfillment fantasy, Jack." So I told him to hitch that fantasy to the back of his Mercedes and leave. He finally did, which left me alone at the house and a bit of an invalid because I had the use of only one arm. I was exhausted; I was tense, frustrated, angry—all at the same time.

I went into the living room, sat in the wing-backed chair and listened to the rain pelting the picture window. I tried hard to think about Erika because I supposed that I should think about her, that it was my duty to think about her. But I couldn't. I'd been thinking about her and talking about her for a week, and I had to turn my attention to something else.

My arm itched—the one in the cast—and I remembered that I could have gotten a long, plastic scratching device to insert under the cast. I tried to ignore the itch.

I remembered that the gutter on the east side of the house still needed fixing. The rain falling two stories from it was forming a deep trough at the edge of the foundation; I got a mental picture of myself getting the ladder out of the garage, carting it back to the house—with my good arm—setting the ladder up against the house, and doing the work. I thought I could even do it in the dark, with the aid of the spotlight, despite the rain.

I thought about Will, too. I thought that I had been telling myself for years that I knew him only too well, and could predict him. I had always realized the intensity of his feeling for Erika, but had been telling myself that because he was such a pragmatic, reasonable, and rational person, he'd never let anyone know about it, especially me. I grinned at that, there in my wing-backed chair. I whispered to myself, "Who, for God's sake, can you know too well?"

Which took me back to Erika, if only for a moment. She unsettled me now. I knew that if she walked into the house and said, "Hi, Jack, I'm back," I wouldn't know what to say to her, that I'd stand for a while looking dumbly at her. And at last I'd say something like, "Hi. What in the hell are you doing here?"

Tiny pellets of sleet got involved with the rain hitting the window. I imagined that it sounded like fingernails, which made me nervous, so I told myself that it sounded more like flies hitting the window, and that reminded me of the flies I'd seen all over the ceiling of the house in Granada. "Asshole," I whispered.

The floor of the front porch was uneven, so whenever someone tried to use the metal storm door leading to this porch, it took lots of effort. On particularly wet days, I'd found the door wouldn't open more than a few inches.

I heard someone fighting with that door as I sat in my wing-backed chair. I heard the harsh scraping sound that the bottom of the door made on the warped porch floor; I felt the house shake very slightly as the door was pushed once, then again.

I got out of the chair, turned around, went into the library, then to the front door, the door that opened onto the porch.

I stood behind the closed front door for several seconds, listened, heard the same scraping noises, felt the house shake a little, heard someone shuffling about. I nearly said, "Who's there?" But I stayed quiet. I listened for another minute, and another. I went back to my chair, closed my eyes.

I said aloud, though not loud enough that whoever was on the porch would have heard me, "Who's there? Please. Who's there?'' But there was no one on the porch, then. The noises had stopped.

I listened to the rain and the sleet hitting the window. I wept. Because I realized how very, very much I wanted Erika back, how much I wanted our routines back, even the occasional boredom, even cleaning up after the cats, and especially sleeping together—curling up naked, my stomach to her back, my thighs against hers, my arm over her. She was the only woman I had ever actually been able to sleep with that way, and I missed it.

I did not believe for a moment that some crazy had gotten hold of her. I believed that she was too smart for that, too wary. And too alive. She was one of those people who looked and acted as if she would *always* be alive—the kind of person that death could never touch. If it tried to touch her, she'd simply slip away, grinning.

I thought that the people around the house were crazy. But I thought they were probably benevolent crazies. Back-to-the-landers. Maybe they slept in quickly built lean-tos, or on the ground in sleeping bags, or even in the trees. People did much stranger things than that. The Cohocton Tree-Sitting Festival was stranger. The middle-aged men who annually dove into the ocean, in February—they called themselves the Polar Bears, I think—were crazier than that. They just didn't carry it out for quite as long as these people had. They weren't as *committed* to their craziness.

In my wing-backed chair, I smiled through my weeping as I peeked at these thoughts, and eventually I said to myself, "Oh, hell, Jack, she'll come home. She always has. Just give her some time."

And I believed it.

The dusk that evening was pigeon-gray, flat, and very quick—it brought the night down with a thud, and the night pulled me out of that chair and led me around the house. *Lock the doors,* it said. *Turn the lights on, turn all the lights on!* it said. So I did. I was beyond the point of feeling embarrassed for my fears. They were rational, after all. Benevolent or otherwise, there were people around the house, in Cohocton, in Dansville, who did strange things, who had probably vandalized the house and who probably had something to do with Erika's disappearance.

At 7:30, Sarah Talpey came to the house.

She looked tired. She was dressed in tan pants, a denim jacket, a white cotton turtleneck shirt, hiking boots. But she looked very tired, at the point of exhaustion, in fact, and I told her so.

"Thanks," she said, grinning, sat down at the kitchen table, and asked if I could make some coffee. I put some water on to boil, sat down across from her at the table. She took a pack of Camel Lights out of her coat pocket.

I said, "I didn't know you smoked, Sarah."

"I used to," she said. "I gave it up ten years ago. I need it again, I'm afraid." She glanced about. "Do you have an ashtray, Jack?"

I got up. In the cupboard under the sink I found an

aluminum foil dish that had once had a Swanson chicken pot pie in it; Erika saved everything. I took the dish back to Sarah and sat down again. I said, "Erika's missing. Did you know that?"

She shook her head. "No. How long?"

"A week. A little more than a week."

"Have you notified anyone?"

"Yes. The police. They said to sit tight."

"Oh. She's done this before, then?"

I nodded. "Once or twice."

She lit a cigarette, took a very long drag of it, coughed once, took another, shorter drag. She coughed again, more severely. "I've forgotten how awful it feels," she said. "I never thought I'd take it up again."

The water started boiling. I stood, hesitated. "I'm glad you're here," I said.

"I had to come here, Jack." She tapped some ashes into the foil dish. "I had to warn you."

I turned off the stove, took the teakettle to the counter. "Oh?" The thoughts I'd once had about her—that she was not unlike Dr. Bernie Swan and his "heavily mutated arachnids"—came back. "Want some cream in your coffee, Sarah?"

"No. Black."

"Sure." Those thoughts stayed, I realized, because I knew it was altogether possible that she was, herself, one of the crazies wandering about.

I brought the coffee back to the table. "Warn me about what, Sarah?"

"About these . . . people, of course." She raised

the cup to her lips and blew on the coffee to cool it. Some of it splattered onto the glass table top; a drop hit her cigarette in the foil dish and caused a slight hissing noise. "I came to warn you about these people. I came to tell you that they might hurt you."

"I know they've got toys in their attic—"

"I don't like that phrase, Jack," she cut in.

"Sorry." I took a nervous sip of my coffee, burned my tongue, took another nervous sip, burned my tongue again.

She shook her head quickly, butted out the half-smoked Camel Light, and fished in the pack for another. "It's a personal problem; that's all. I didn't mean to snap at you."

I smiled. "Don't worry about it." I took another, slower sip of coffee and let it slide under my tongue. It tasted awful. "So tell me who these people are, Sarah."

"They're not *people*. I can tell you that. They're not *people*." She lit another cigarette, butted it out immediately, got another from the pack, lit it, smiled. "I mean that quite literally, Jack." She took a quick puff of the cigarette, butted it out. "I'm trying to quit," she said, as if as an aside.

"You should," I told her.

"I will. Right now." And she crumpled the pack into a wad the size of a Ping-Pong ball. "Wastebasket?" she said; I nodded backwards. She leaned to her right, and tossed the crumpled cigarette pack expertly so it landed in a grocery bag I'd set up in a corner of the kitchen. "I played basketball once," she said, and grinned.

"Good for you," I said.

"You don't believe me, do you?"

"About playing basketball?"

"Please don't be an idiot, Jack. It doesn't suit you."

"Thanks," I said. "No, I don't believe you."

She took a long swig of the coffee and set the cup down hard on the table. "I know they *look* like people—"

I interrupted, "*Just* like people, Sarah. Hands and feet and heads and everything."

She looked me squarely in the eye. "Continue patronizing me, Jack, and I'll leave. Do you want me to leave?"

I said immediately, and meant it, "No. I'm sorry. I want you to stay."

She went over to the grocery bag, retrieved the crumpled cigarette pack, straightened it out, got a smashed cigarette from it, examined it. At last she came back to the table and lit the cigarette. "I don't always act this way, Jack." Smoke came out of several tears in the cigarette, so she drew harder. "I'm a little nervous tonight. I'm very nervous."

"That's obvious, Sarah."

"I'm being a real twitch, aren't I?"

"Yes."

"Would you like to know *where* these people come from, Jack?"

"I'm sure you're going to tell me," I said.

"They come from the earth." She pointed stiffly at the floor. "From there. From the earth." She smiled thinly, took a long sip of her coffee and set the cup down. "They come from the *earth*, Jack."

I looked quietly at her for a moment. Then I said, "Sarah—*I* come from the earth. We *all* come from the earth!"

"Not quite as directly as they do, Jack."

"Oh? What does that mean?"

"It means that they *sprang* from it, Jack. Like the trees did. And the mushrooms. And the azaleas." She took another long, slow, very satisfied sip of the coffee. "And I'll make a confession, too." She set the cup down. "I've been wanting to tell that to someone for a very long time. I mean—it's not a *theory*, it's not my pet theory. It's a fact. Like this table." She hit it with her fist, spilling some of her coffee. "And like that!" She pointed happily at the spill. "A fact. Accept it, don't accept it, *they* don't care!

"Jack, there are snakes with two heads, and there are fourteen-hundred-pound men, and amino acids in meteorites that have fallen in China, and there are people, here, around this house, who sprang up from the earth. Like mushrooms."

"Or azaleas?"

"Yes!"

"Are you one of them, Sarah?"

She grinned at that, flicked the ash off the torn cigarette she'd been smoking, shrugged. "I could be. Hell, *you* could be, Jack. I don't think that I am. I can recall a past, a childhood. I remember standing up in my crib when I was two or three years old and being frightened by some neighborhood boys peeking in the window. But those could be manufactured memories, and I think it would probably be very difficult to tell the difference between manufactured memories and real ones.''

"Yes, I've heard that theory."

"I'm sure you have." A pause. When she went on, her tone was softer. "I would dearly love to be one of them. Of course. What more could a naturalist wish for than to be a creature of the earth,''—she looked earnestly at me—"a *creation* of the earth. Like the things that she studies—"

I cut in, "Carry it a little bit further, Sarah. Gee, an auto mechanic could be a car, a writer a book, a beekeeper a bee—"

She stood abruptly, stalked to the door, opened it, hesitated, looked around at me. She said, her voice quaking, "And now they're going *back* to the earth, Jack. That's what I believe. They're going *back* to the earth." She looked expectantly at me, was obviously waiting for a reply.

"I'm sorry," I told her. "Really, Sarah, I'm very sorry, but I have other things to think about."

She said, her voice steady now, "No, Jack, I'm afraid you don't." And she left the house.

Erika and I went to Durand Eastman Park, near Lake Ontario, several years after we were married. We'd gone into Rochester to visit my mother, and decided we'd have a picnic and take a swim before driving back to Syracuse. We packed hot dogs, some macaroni and potato salad, baked beans, rolls, mustard, relish, and when we got to the park, we went for a swim first.

She is an excellent swimmer, much at home in the water, as if it is her second element, and we swam for a good hour together.

The beach was not terribly crowded. There were some children near where we'd set our towel down. They were playing a clumsy game of volleyball, *sans* net. Several yards on the other side of us a couple in their teens were busily fondling each other.

After swimming we sat on the beach together. We talked about my mother—Erika has always liked her, although my mother makes it clear that Erika should not get *too* close—and about the day—very warm and bright—about politics, though briefly. After a while I became aware that Erika was growing agitated, that her gaze was shifting from me to the young couple who'd been fondling each other. I looked. They'd stopped fondling each other. The boy was covering the girl with sand.

I asked Erika if something was wrong. She said no, though the strain and agitation was obvious in her tone.

I nodded at the couple, who were oblivious to us: "Does that bother you, Erika?"

"Why should it bother me, Jack? No. Of course it doesn't bother me." But it was clear, as the sand continued to cover the girl, that Erika was becoming increasingly agitated.

"Let's go eat," I suggested. I thought, at that point, that Erika was on the verge of saying something to the young couple, and of course, I wanted to avoid that.

She looked quickly at me. "I'm not hungry, Jack."

"Well, we've got to get the fire started—"

She looked at the young couple. She said to them, though low enough that they didn't hear her, "Why are you doing that?"

"Erika," I said, "please, it's nothing—"

"Don't *do* that!" she hollered at them.

The boy looked over, astonished; then the girl. "Huh?" said the boy.

"Why are you *doing* that?" Erika asked, her voice sharp and high-pitched.

"Somethin' wrong with you, lady?"

"No," I said to him, "we're sorry; nothing's wrong."

"Don't *do* that to her!" Erika hollered.

"Erika, let's go." I stood, leaned over, tried to pull her to a standing position. She wouldn't budge.

"Erika, please—"

She screamed. It was long, shrill, and completely unexpected, of course. The couple near us jumped to their feet. The boy muttered several low and violent curses, and they ran off.

I stared at Erika for a good long time. She did not scream again. She stared quietly at the lake, and at last I sat down next to her and asked her why she'd screamed.

She shook her head. "Just dreams," she said.

"I don't understand," I said.

"I don't either."

And that's where we left it.

CHAPTER TWENTY-ONE

I should have felt badly about driving Sarah Talpey away, but then, that night, while I sat at the kitchen table and watched her leave, and for the rest of the evening, I could afford to feel badly about nothing. I could afford to feel very little because I was being battered on all sides, because my life had gone topsy-turvy and the best I could do for myself, at that moment, was to put everything aside, as I'd been trying to do before Sarah arrived.

I decided to paint the kitchen. Erika and I had discussed painting it when we first moved to the house. It was an ugly dark yellow, streaked with age, and though the kitchen was twice the size of most kitchens, that color made it feel like a cave.

We'd bought some paint a month earlier, a pretty light blue that C. R. Boring swore would cover anything in just one coat. I got a gallon of it out of a closet in the laundry room—where we stored tools, paint, and the vacuum cleaner—took it into the kitchen, went back to the closet for a roller, a pan, and a stick to stir the paint with. With one hand, it took several trips. And when I was done and all the painting paraphernalia was neatly in place on the kitchen table, I asked myself, "What the hell am I doing?" And I put it all away and went to bed.

That was at about eight o'clock.

It was at one o'clock that Erika's voice broke into a particularly cold and nasty dream. "Jack?" I heard, her tone soft and casual, as if she were going to ask me what time it was. I struggled out of the dream, heard "Jack?" again, followed by "Are you here?" I woke, pushed myself up on my good elbow in the bed.

"Yes, Erika, I am," I said. The overhead light was on, the door open. I remembered closing the door, remembered turning the light off. I swung my feet to the floor, felt a deep, sharp pain in my shoulder, winced, let out a little groan, heard beneath it: "Jack?" The pain stopped.

"Erika?" I stood, went to the door, and looked out into the big, open room at the top of the stairs. The overhead light was on here, too; I had left it on as a sort of night-light. "Erika?" I called, listened a moment, called to her again, and again. Listened. Heard nothing. "Erika, please—"

"Jack?" I heard, very faintly, from the back of the house.

"Erika!" I called, urgently now, and made my way quickly through the open room, into the bathroom behind it, and then into the L-shaped and cluttered spare room. I flicked the light on. "Erika?" I said. "Erika, are you in here?"

"Yes," I heard.

But the room was empty.

"Where are you?" I called; I heard tension, frustration, and anger in my voice. "Christ, Erika, where are you?"

I stood in that room for an hour or more, listening for her, saying her name.

At last I went back to the bedroom, turned the light off, climbed into the bed. "My God, Erika," I whispered into the darkness. "My God, I love you."

Daylight was all over the room when I woke. I muttered an obscenity at it, got reluctantly out of bed, and cursed again, this time at the pain in my shoulder. It was very localized now, like a toothache, and at times it was all but unbearable. I went to the east-facing window and looked out at the driveway, hoping to see Erika's blue Volvo there, hoping that she'd decided, at last, to come back to me, as she had a half-dozen times before.

At the road a young, dark-haired man was walking

slowly, hands thrust into his pants pockets, head lowered. He was talking to himself. I could see his mouth move and his head shake now and then, as if he were in disagreement with someone. An old Buick Electra that was caked with mud and loaded with people passed him as I watched. It slowed as it approached him. A rear window was lowered, and a square, middle-aged face appeared that looked as if it were cackling. The Electra veered toward the young man then, and I heard the long, coarse wail of its horn, followed by the squeal of its tires as it accelerated. The young man didn't flinch. I thought, *Some people around here are fucking crazy!* and straightened from the window, cursed again at a moment of pain in my shoulder, turned, and saw movement in the big, open room that adjoined the bedroom.

"Who's there?" I said. I heard a heavy thumping noise, as if someone had backed into a wall. I went quickly through the bedroom so I was close to the door, hesitated, said again, "Who's there?" and heard someone weeping very softly, as if from within a closed room. "Erika?" I said. The weeping came to a slow stop. I left the bedroom, went into the open room, said her name again and again. I even looked closely at the corners of the room, as if she might have been huddling in shadow.

"Erika," I pleaded at last, "for Christ's sake, what are you doing?"

* * *

Jerry Czech came to the house an hour later. He'd picked up my Toyota while I was in the hospital. When I answered the door, he nodded toward the driveway and announced, "She's done, Mr. Harris." I looked where he'd nodded. The Toyota was in the driveway behind his tow truck. The top was still caved in slightly, the left front fender folded back six inches or so.

"Good," I said. "What's the damage?"

"I fixed the damage," he explained confusedly. "Fixed it good's I could, anyway. You turn a car over and you're usually gonna have some damage that's gonna show—"

I interrupted, "No. I'm sorry. What I meant was, how much do I owe you?"

"Seven hundred'll do 'er."

"Seven hundred dollars?" I was incredulous.

"That's the damage. Sure." He grinned.

"My God, what did you do to it?"

"I put a new engine in it. Wasn't a *new* engine; no, wasn't a *new* engine. It was a *old* engine, but it worked. Yers didn't work. Yers had a busted block so it didn't work."

"You should have called me—"

"Your wife said it was okay. I wouldn'ta done it but your wife said it was okay—"

"My wife?"

"Sure. Mrs. Harris. She said it was okay."

"When?" I tried to control my anxiety.

"When I fixed your car."

"Christ, I *know* that. I meant when did you *see* her; when did you talk to my wife?"

"Coupla days ago. When I picked your car up. Toyota's a good car—"

"Who was she with?" I cut in.

"No one. A man. Some man. He wasn't really with her. He was around, I guess. Just around. And I thought he was with her. You could ask her, you know. I mean, if she's stepping out on ya—"

"What did he look like?"

"I don't know. Why should I know? He looked like the rest of 'em, I guess; I dunno."

I nodded impatiently at the car. "Will you take a check?"

"I'll take a check, sure. If it's good."

I drove into Cohocton an hour later. Driving with only one good arm would have been an easy task under normal conditions, but a light rain had started, and a heavy overcast had cut the daylight in half. So when, a quarter mile from the house, I rounded a hill and saw a group of five or six people walking toward me down the center of my lane, I steered quickly to the left, lost my grip on the wheel, grabbed it again, hit the brake too hard, started skidding on the wet pavement, and shot past them with little room to spare. I spent a long time cursing them, cursing the car, myself, my bad shoulder, Jerry Czech. And yes, Erika. I had these people figured out, you see. They were like Moonies. They were fanatics of one sort or another. Religious fanatics or not, it didn't much matter. They'd seduced Erika away from me. They'd made her an offer she couldn't refuse. Eternal happiness. Inner peace. It didn't matter. I wanted her back, and I was going to find her and bring her home.

I chalked this up as a distinct possibility: They were convinced, as a group, that they were what Sarah had told me they were—creatures of the earth— that they were creatures the earth had produced. And now they were equally convinced that the earth was somehow calling them back. That was rational, and believable. I began to believe it. I knew very little about them, only what I had seen in Granada (which, upon reflection, began to spook the hell out of me) and what I had seen in Seth's eyes—distance, and confusion. And fear.

They were everywhere that morning, like deer on a rainy spring night. They were on the road, in the fields to the sides of the road, milling about the several empty and abandoned houses on the way to Cohocton. I stopped once to talk to one of them, a young woman in a blue dress, beige sandals, and white sweater. She was standing at the side of the road, soaked by the rain, facing away from me, and when I pulled up beside her, I had to lean over and roll the passenger window down. "Hello," I said, which got no reaction, so I said it again, louder, more angrily, and because it still got no reaction, I said it once more, and added, "Goddamnit!" That got no reaction, either. I thought a moment. I asked, "What are you doing here?" Nothing. "What in the *fuck* are you doing here?'' I insisted. She'd been standing with her hands at her sides. She appeared to cross her arms now—I couldn't be sure because she was facing away from me—and walked off slowly through the mud at the side of the road, one slow step at a time, so, with each step, her foot could relax and free itself from the mud, into a stand of aspens near the road, through them, up a slight hill, and then into deep brush beyond. I stared for some time in the direction she'd gone. At last I turned back and floored the accelerator. I got to Cohocton minutes later.

I knew only a few of the townies. Knebel—who had once warned me about ''people standing by themselves, in the dark''—C. R. Boring, Ulla Perrson, Larry Whipple, the deputy sheriff, and Jean, a red-haired, thirtyish, matronly woman who worked as a clerk at the post office. There were several other people whom I didn't know by name but who nodded at me when they saw me on the street. I'd come to the conclusion that Cohocton was a typical small town with small town attitudes. Shortly after we'd moved in, Erwin ''Bud'' Huber, Cohocton's mayor, made a proposal that ''all pornography be forever prohibited from sale, public or private, in our lovely little town'' because, he explained, ''people in Cohocton live on a higher plane.'' Never mind that the closest thing to pornography available in Cohocton, anyway, was a particularly graphic wrestling magazine: ''The idea,'' he explained, ''is to stop this cancer at its source.'' The proposal drew national attention not only because it was typically small townish, and therefore had lots of human interest potential, but also because it was so blatantly unconstitutional. Eventually it became an embarrassment, and the town trustees let it die.

And because Cohocton was so typically a small town, I was certain its people would have rallied around this new problem.

Here's the scenario I expected: Small groups of townies would have formed here and there—in front of Boring's, in front of the bank, the post office, the IGA. These groups would be discussing the current problem. The discussions would be reasonable, on balance. A few hotheads—like the people in the Electra—might try to run the show, but sweet reason (and that, after all, is what keeps towns like Cohocton together) would prevail and the hotheads would be asked to go somewhere else. Erwin "Bud" Huber would be flitting from group to group, but since the pornography amendment had blown up in his face, he'd be graciously ignored. The thread running through these groups would be an awareness that although the strange people who'd come to the town—or at least to the areas surrounding it—seemed placid enough, and although they did little or nothing that was illegal, they represented an unknown presence and were therefore not to be trusted. At last, the groups would begin to tie together; the one at the IGA would wander over and join the group at the post office. They would, in turn, attract the group at the hardware store, which would, finally, attract the last group. Someone would take charge (and I was hoping that that someone would be me). He'd give the situation a very thorough and reasoned analysis, and then, in the time-honored tradition of all small towns, propose that a vote be taken to decide what to do next.

But the streets of Cohocton were all but empty that morning. A Datsun pickup was parked in front of the post office, and a battered Ford station wagon, its hood up, stood in the IGA parking lot. A young woman carrying a screeching infant on her back was walking slowly through the light rain, smiling— apparently mindless of her wailing child—toward the Cohocton Hotel.

I parked in front of the bank, across the street from the Datsun pickup. When I got out, I heard from behind me, "Jack, hello." I turned. It was Knebel. He'd apparently just come around the corner of the bank—the alley there leads to his apartment—and was tugging his old German shepherd along.

"Hi," I called. He was still a good twenty feet from me. I gestured to indicate the town. "Quiet, isn't it?"

He smiled, had clearly not heard me.

I repeated, "Quiet, isn't it, Knebel?!"

"Hi," he called—apparently he had still not heard me—and then he stopped because his dog refused to go on.

I walked over to him, noticed around him the strong, unpleasant odor of the little cigars he smoked. I patted the dog. "He's pretty old, isn't he, Knebel?"

"Close to fifteen. Haven't seen you in a while, Jack." He nodded at the cast on my arm. "Broke your shoulder, huh?"

"Cracked it."

"Oh? I heard it was broken." He smiled. "Small town gossip, very unreliable. Got your Toyota fixed, I see. Good car, those Toyotas. They last forever."

I gestured again. "Why's it so quiet, here?"

"Everyone's at the carnival in Penn Yann. 'Cept me, of course." His dog lifted a leg and started cleaning itself. Knebel leaned over, pushed the leg down. "No, Hans," he whispered. "Later."

I said, "My wife's missing, Knebel."

He looked up from his dog, nodded, looked back; the dog was cleaning itself again. "I know that. Left you for those religious fanatics, I hear. Bad luck, Jack."

His casual attitude made me instantly angry. "Christ, Knebel, it's more than bad luck—" I stopped, aware of my anger.

He looked up and grinned. "No need to get upset, Jack. My daughter left us for some religious fanatics in Utah. Not the Mormons. Some other group. So I know what it's like, believe me. I feel for you, but what can I do about it?"

"The question is, Knebel, what can we *all* do about it?"

" 'All,' Jack? Who's *all*?"

"The people. Here. The people in Cohocton."

"What do you want them to do, Jack?"

I hesitated. It was a good question. I shook my

head a little. "I don't know." I remembered my scenario. "I don't know," I repeated. "I guess we could all get together and talk about it."

"Talk about what?"

"About the situation, for Christ's sake."

"You're getting upset again, Jack." He leaned over, pushed his dog's leg down once more. "Not now, damnit!" he whispered. He looked up at me. "Besides, what situation are you talking about?"

"About these religious fanatics, of course."

Knebel shrugged. "Who are they hurting? So they're all over the place?! There's not much anyone can do about that, short of running 'em out of town." He grinned. "And no one can do that, can they? You just watch out for them, Jack. You try not to run 'em down. And if you want, you go looking for whoever it is they took away from you. That's my advice. They took Erika away from you?" He shrugged again. "Well, you go and get her. Course, you got to know where to look, and that could be a problem, I guess." He pushed at Hans's leg again, whispered an obscenity, looked back at me. "Seen this, Jack?" He nodded to indicate the dog's collar. I looked. It had a series of small lights set around it; the lights were variously blue, green, red, and they were flashing rhythmically. Knebel continued, "My own invention, Jack? Works with a battery pack." He lifted a small brown box hanging from the collar. "Here."

I shook my head slightly. "Sure, Knebel," I whispered. "I'll see you again, okay?" and without waiting for an answer I turned and walked away from him.

I heard him call behind me, "Hey, good luck there, Jack. Don't get yourself converted."

CHAPTER TWENTY-TWO

Jean, the thirtyish, matronly woman at the post office, said, "Live and let live, Mr. Harris. You know, I've got that on a plaque in my living room, and I really do believe it; I live by it." A short pause for effect. "We *all* should, don't you think?" She smiled a big self-satisfied smile. "Stamps, Mr. Harris?"

"No," I said. "Thank you." And I left.

In the hardware store, C. R. Boring was seated on a tall metal stool behind the counter. He looked happy to see a customer come in. "I like carnivals as much as the next guy, Mr. Ferris—" he began.

"Harris," I corrected.

"Yes?" Momentary confusion. "And this one in Penn Yann is a doozy, but there's no sense abandoning Cohocton. What's the businessman going to do, Mr. Harris? Which of us can afford to lose a day's worth of business? These are hard times."

"Don't those others shop here?"

He adjusted himself on his metal stool, crossed his legs. He looked very uncomfortable. "You mean these hippies, don't you?"

I nodded.

"I wish they did. But they don't. One of 'em came in here, once. I asked him what he wanted, he didn't answer, so I asked him again, and he wandered out without so much as a 'How ya do?' Damned spooky sons of bitches—"

"My feelings exactly," I cut in, my tone dripping with meaning.

"Like bats," he said, and grimaced. "I hate bats. I know they're not gonna hurt no one. You live here long's I have you get to know what's going to hurt you and what isn't. Bat's not going to hurt anyone. A two-ounce flying mouse with a taste for insects, that's all your basic bat is. But, by God, they scare the piss outa me, Mr. Harris."

I smiled knowingly. "Just like these people do."

"Sure," he said.

"Me, too."

"But they're harmless."

I shook my head. "Are they, Mr. Boring? Are they really harmless?"

"Charlie. That's my first name. I don't much care for being called Mr. Boring."

"Oh. Yes. I'm sorry."

"So what can I do for you today? You finally fixing that gutter of yours? I got some good plastic gutter that'll last from now till doomsday—"

"We're getting off the subject here, Charlie."

"What was the subject?"

"These people."

"Oh. Sure. The hippies. Shoot 'em."

" 'Shoot 'em'?"

"Sure." He smiled secretively, leaned over, whispered, "You take this"—he pulled a small pistol from under the counter, held it up for me to see—"it's only a .22 caliber, but if you put it right up against a person's temple, you can drop 'em good, and then you dig yourself a great big hole and you dump 'em all in it. It's what I do with the bats, Mr. Harris. I know where they live, you see, and I go there and I kill maybe a hundred, two hundred of 'em—"

"Good Christ," I whispered, and backed away from him.

He was still smiling. "You wanta come with me sometime? I think you'd like it. And if you ever wanta do that, if you ever wanta drill these hippies, you come here and I'll go with ya. Wouldn't like nothin' better than to drill these hippies. Remember Kent State, Mr. Harris? 1970?"

I pulled the door open and left. I thought, as I had

thought about my brother, *Who can you know too well?*

I went to the bank. There were no customers there, and only three tellers—a thin, middle-aged woman in a white blouse and pleated orange skirt, an attractive woman of twenty-five or so wearing a blue pants suit, and a fat man in his sixties who was wearing a gray pin-striped suit and looked very much as if he would rather have been somewhere else.

The young woman looked over when I came in; she smiled appealingly and said, "Good morning. May I help you?"

I grinned, shook my head. "No."

She looked disappointed.

"I wanted to talk," I went on.

"Oh?" she said, and looked confused.

I heard the door open behind me and I stepped out of the way. A scruffy, unshaven man of about forty-five, who smelled vaguely of cigarettes and cow manure, came in. He was counting a stack of bills— "Four hundred twenty," he whispered, "four hundred thirty, thirty-five . . ."

"May I help you?" the young woman said to him, and he went over to her, pushed the stack of bills at her, asked her to count it, told her he wanted to make a deposit.

I went over to the middle-aged woman, said "Hi."

"Hello," she said coolly.

"I wanted to talk," I said.

"Beautiful morning," she said.

"No," I said. "It's been raining."

"Rain's good."

"Uh-huh." I fished my wallet out of my back pocket, withdrew thirty dollars, said I wanted to make a deposit.

"Deposit slips are over there," she said, and nodded at a table behind me.

"I don't know my account number," I said.

"We can look it up. Your name is?"

I told her my name. Then I added, "Actually, I just wanted to talk."

"You don't want to make a deposit, Mr. Harris?" She looked suspiciously at me.

"Sure, I'll make a deposit."

"I'll get your account number, then. Deposit slips are over there," and again she nodded at the table behind me.

"Yes," I said. "In a moment. I wanted to talk about these people wandering about."

The older man at the next teller's cage said loudly, "Bring back the loitering laws, that's my solution. Then you can throw those bums in the slammer. That'll get rid of 'em."

And the scruffy man making the large deposit said, "Steal my corn and they'll get their fannies fulla buckshot."

The young woman looked offended, but said nothing.

The middle-aged woman waiting on me said, "My son hitchhiked to Wyoming once, and he did what I guess these people do—he slept where he could, under the stars, and that's okay. Brings a person closer to God.''

''I think they're religious fanatics,'' I said, which got several moments of stiff silence. Then the scruffy man announced, ''I'm a Bible Baptist, young man, and we ain't fanatics.''

''No,'' I said, my tone apologetic, ''I was talking about these people wandering the countryside. I think they've taken my wife.'' I felt good saying that, as if I'd gotten over the hump of the conversation.

''Taken her where?'' asked the middle-aged woman.

''They've seduced her away from me.''

The fat man said, ''That's an aberration; these religious groups are moving into untried areas, like sex . . .''

The young woman said, ''Sex is hardly an 'untried area,' Lou.''

''They're probably all fucking their brains out in the woods,'' Lou said.

''Ladies are present,'' the scruffy man admonished. Lou apologized.

The middle-aged woman said, ''If she's a consenting adult, Mr. Harris, then she is at liberty to go where she pleases and with whom she pleases. Your savings account has been closed; would you like to open a new one?''

''It's been closed? I never closed it.''

''No. Your wife did. Several days ago. When you were still in the hospital, I think. How's your arm, by the way?''

I ignored the question. ''Who was she with?''

"She was by herself, Mr. Harris." She paused. "I think there was someone waiting outside for her. A man about your age, maybe. Would you like to reopen the account?"

"No. Thank you." I turned to leave; Lou, the fat teller, called after me, "Once deer season opens, these hippies will go away, couple of 'em get shot. You wait and see." And he grinned knowingly.

"No one's gonna get shot," the scruffy man said.

"Someone always gets shot," the young woman said.

I turned back. "My God," I said stiffly, "none of you people sees the *importance* of this thing. My God, you don't even care, do you?"

"Mister Harris," Lou said, "there's no *problem*. And if a problem should develop, we'll deal with it."

"I don't even *live* here," the young woman said. "I live in Canandaigua, and we don't have a problem there."

"What can we do with these people, anyway?" asked the middle-aged woman. "You can't just tell them to go away. It's a free country, Mr. Harris."

"Oh, for God's sake—"

She cut in, "Your wife didn't look at all unhappy, either. I think it's important that you realize that. She was smiling, in fact."

"That makes me *very* happy," I said, my tone thick with sarcasm.

"Just trying to be . . ." the woman said, but I was out the door before she finished the sentence.

*   *   *

I went looking for Erika myself. I drove down Hunt's Hollow Road, past the house, past Wildwood Farms, two miles north of the house, drove another half mile and parked the car on the shoulder of the road. The rain had stopped, but the shoulder was several inches deep in mud and I thought I'd have trouble getting the car out of it.

I made my way into a shallow gully just off the shoulder, climbed up the other side, pushed into some thick brush there, and fifty feet in came to Old Hunt's Hollow Road, which hadn't been used for over fifty years and was overgrown with grasses and birch trees that sprang up after a forest fire thirty years earlier.

I stopped at the center of this road, looked right and left; I saw very little except the occasional movement of birds. Then, surprising myself, I yelled, "Erika?" I heard anger in my voice. "Erika, goddamnit!" The words came back to me. Once. Then again. And again several seconds later. I remember thinking what a weird kind of echo it was, so I yelled once more, intrigued. "Erika, goddamnit!" and the words came back to me from several places—from Hunt's Hollow Road a hundred feet to my right, from deep within the thickets to my left, from behind me, and up. I turned and looked. Old Hunt's Hollow Road gave itself over to a thick growth of red dogwood and sumac that grew on a small hill fifty yards away. The top of this hill was just visible through the vegetation. And as I looked, I heard "Goddamnit,

Erika!'' in my voice, and I thought again, *This is a fucking weird kind of echo*.

"Goddamnit, goddamnit!" I heard, still in my voice, and I whispered, "What the hell is going on here?" That came back to me, too, in the same stiff whisper, but as if there were a crowd of people hiding around me, repeating it. "What the hell is going on here?" I heard. Then, as if in afterthought, "Erika?" And a moment later, "Goddamnit!"

"This is fucking weird," I said.

"This is fucking weird, Erika," I heard. "Goddamnit, goddamnit, this is fucking weird!"

"What the *hell* is going on here?"

"What the *hell*, goddamnit, Erika, goddamnit, what the hell, goddamnit, is going on, Erika, goddamnit, what the hell is going on, this is fucking weird, here, goddamnit, what the *hell* is going on here, Erika, what the *hell* . . ." It was a chorus of shouts and whispers that I heard now, from many directions, as I turned tight little circles at the center of Old Hunt's Hollow Road, as I tried desperately, and in vain, to see something other than dogwood, sumac, maple, and birch, the movement of birds, an occasional glimpse of blue sky.

Then, like frogs startled by noise, the voices stopped all at once.

"Erika?" I said. "Are you there, Erika?" Silence. "Erika, come back home; come home with me? We've got things to do—the roof needs fixing; the gutter needs fixing; the front door sticks." Far to my right, in the direction of the house, a big raccoon ambled across

Old Hunt's Hollow Road. On a lone wooden fence post close to me a white-faced hornet took flight, circled me once, then again, and was gone. The air had become still, humid, and warm in the last half hour.

I called, "Hey, Erika?" and waited a moment, heard nothing, added, "I love you," felt a little embarrassed smile start, dissipate, said again, louder, "I love you!" and knew that, out of desperation, frustration, and anger, I was on the verge of shouting it. But I didn't shout it. I turned and pushed my way back through the thickets to the car, had some trouble getting it out of the mud at the shoulder, but finally did it with some skillful use of the clutch and accelerator, and on the short drive back to the house said over and over again, "Goddamn religious fanatics, goddamn religious fanatics!"

It was not until later, upon reflection, that I realized the roads had been empty.

CHAPTER TWENTY-THREE

Will came to the house that evening. He stood sheepishly at the front door and said, "Can I come in?" I said of course he could and showed him into the dining room, asked if he'd like anything. "No," he answered, thought a moment, and added, "I've never felt quite so foolish, Jack."

"No need," I said.

He sat at the head of the table. I stood, arms folded, near the door to the library, my back to the wall.

I continued, "I understand why you said it, Will,"

referring to his comment that Erika was "still in the house somewhere."

"Do you?" he said, and looked confusedly at me.

"Yes." I didn't want to elaborate. I launched into my theory that the people around the house were religious fanatics. He stopped me in mid-monologue.

"Sure," he said, "but where'd they go, Jack?"

"Where'd they go?"

"They're not there anymore."

"Sure they are."

"No, Jack. I saw some deer on my way down. I saw a raccoon—I almost hit it, as a matter of fact—and I think I saw a few bats. But I didn't see any of those people. I think they went home, Jack—wherever that is."

I shook my head. "They were everywhere this afternoon. I went looking for Erika, Will. And they were everywhere." I stopped, remembered driving back from Cohocton, passing the house, parking the car on the shoulder, driving back to the house. I shook my head again, in confusion now. "I'm *sure* they were," I whispered.

"They're not there anymore," Will said, paused, went on, his tone low, as if he were speaking in confidence, "You think they've got her, don't you?"

"Yes," I said. "Of course they do."

He leaned forward, put his elbows on the table, and folded his hands in front of his face. He said, eyes straight ahead, "Okay, so when she gets tired of them, she'll come back to us."

I said nothing.

"She *will* come back to us, Jack."

" 'Us'?" I said.

He was quiet for a moment; then he shrugged as if his remark had been merely casual. "Sure," he said. "She'll come back to us. In time."

I sighed, crossed to the window that overlooked the side yard, and parted the curtains slightly with my hand. The spotlight was on—I didn't remember turning it on—and in its light I could see an opossum trundling off toward the mountain behind the house. The opossum had its own peculiar hitching walk, probably from tangling with a car, so I recognized it as one that Erika had been leaving food for on certain nights. I watched it until it was beyond the perimeter of the spotlight. "Is that why you came here tonight, Will?" I turned my head to look at him. "To apologize?"

"No," he answered at once, and paused.

"Go on," I coaxed.

"Uh-huh," he said, and nodded as if in resignation.

I sat at the table. "What's going on, Will? Why'd you come here tonight?"

He shook his head and grimaced a little, as if at a bad taste. At last he said, "I talked with Erika, Jack. I talked with her today." Another pause. I could say nothing. At last he continued, "You weren't here. I came to see you, but you weren't here. Where were you?"

"Stick to the subject, Will."

He nodded again, said, "Sure," smiled quickly at me, then looked back at his hands still folded in front of him. "She was here, Jack."

"Here? You mean she was in the house?"

He shook his head. "No." He shook his head again, as if for emphasis. "No. She was outside." He lifted his chin slightly to indicate the side yard. "She was out there, just inside the woods. Christ, she scared the hell out of me, Jack. I was coming up to the door, and I heard, 'Hello, Will.' I stopped and I looked around because I recognized her voice, of course—I could hardly hear it, but I recognized it." He paused again, briefly. "I called to her. I didn't know where she might be because I had heard her say only that one thing, so I called to her a couple times. Then she said my name again and I turned and saw her." He lifted his head once more to indicate the same area. "Just inside the woods, Jack. She was standing just inside the woods. And when I saw her, I said something like, 'Good Lord—Erika!' and I started for her." He looked confused, went on, "I can't explain this, Jack. I don't know how to explain this. But when I started for her, when I took a couple of steps toward her"—he shook his head—"she wasn't there. I mean, I kept my eyes on her while I was walking toward her; I kept my eyes on her, and I was smiling, of course, because I was happy to see her. And maybe *because* I was smiling, because I was so very happy to see her . . . I don't know, I was crying too, and when you're crying"—he was on the verge of incoherence now—"it's very hard to *see*, isn't it? I mean, you're not concentrating on seeing, you're concentrating on *crying!* So I think she must have just . . . stepped back into the woods because I became aware—I looked, and I became aware—that she just wasn't *there* anymore."

"You went looking for her, didn't you, Will?"

"Jesus, yes, I looked for her. I looked for an hour and a half. I didn't find her; hell, I called to her over and over again, and I kept telling myself that I could hear *something*; I didn't know what it was, Jack, but it wasn't her, then I finally convinced myself that I'd been seeing things. Why not? Everyone sees things, don't they? I convinced myself that because I"—he looked down self-consciously at the table—"because I do love her, Jack"—he looked up, grinned an apology—"that I'd kind of conjured her up out of the trees and the bushes and the rain." He shrugged. "I can't say it's impossible. I've done stranger things. It was a sort of wish-fulfillment fantasy, Jack." Another grin of apology.

"I understand," I told him.

"I wanted to see her, so I saw her. That's pretty simple, isn't it?"

"Sure it is, Will."

"You don't believe me, do you?"

"Don't believe what?"

"That I saw her. You don't believe I saw her."

"I don't think *you* believe it, Will."

He shook his head, smiled sadly. "I've thought about this, Jack. Ever since it happened I've thought about it. And I *know* that I saw her. She was there. And then she wasn't. It's as simple as that."

I sighed. I didn't know what to say to him.

"I saw her," he repeated, as much to himself as to me. "And Christ, Jack—it was like seeing a ghost."

Book Two

CHAPTER ONE

This turns out to be Erika's story.

Will's story, too.

And Knebel's, Sarah's, mine; the several hundred people who called Cohocton their home.

But mostly it turns out to be Erika's story.

Our memories haunt us. Mostly, they haunt us. We can peer at them and smile and say that they feel good. But they recall the past, which is what it is, and so our memories haunt us. It's all our memories can do, ultimately.

We want to be rational. We take photographs, movies; we write in our journals every day or every couple of days. And for the sake of the future we do the things that need doing. We fix the gutters because the rain that plummets from them will undermine the foundation after a time. We repair the roof; we replace some tiles here and there; we check for dry rot because we know if we don't the house will fall down around us in a few decades. We live for what will be. And we live for what might be.

Sarah Talpey said, "There are snakes with two heads, and there are fourteen-hundred-pound men, and amino acids in meteorites that have fallen in China." And those are the things that are really important.

That night, after Will left and before I went up to bed, I made sure all the doors were unlocked. I said to myself, *She might have lost her keys. She'll have no way in if she's lost her keys.* I checked each door from the outside, and then I went down to Hunt's Hollow Road, in the darkness, and called for her. I got no answer, of course, and what I could see of the road was empty, but I kept calling. Not out of desperation, and not out of anger or futility, but because, for the first time, I believed that she *was* there, near the house. And I was calling to her as if she knew I was calling and she only needed a little time to answer. Perhaps until she got tired of being away from me—a few minutes, or a few hours, or a few days. Longer, maybe. I was letting her know

that I was still interested. "I'm still interested, Erika!"
Silence. "I still love you." Silence. "The doors are
unlocked. There's nothing I'd like better than to
wake and find you beside me." Silence. "That would
be a real treat. I'd like that. We could talk. I think
we need to talk." Silence. "Do you want anything?
A coat? A pair of gloves?" I was grasping now.
"You must be getting awfully hungry. Come back;
I'll feed you." Still nothing. "What do they do for
you, Erika? What's the attraction?" I smiled as if she
were there beside me and I was trying to put her at
ease. "What do they do for you that I don't?" I
shrugged in the darkness. "Hey, I'm sorry." I could
feel myself slipping into a pose. "Everything has to
revolve around *me*, right, Erika? How many times
have you told me that? And it's true—it's been true—
but that will change." I peered into the darkness.
There was a heavy cloud cover, so the darkness was
nearly total. "We'll talk about you, Erika. We'll talk
about *your* needs, finally." Another smile, one of
invitation—*Go ahead*, it said, *talk about yourself.* I
waited, heard nothing, saw nothing, began to feel
foolish, and cold, realized that I had to use the
bathroom. "Erika?" I called at last, "I'm going into
the house now. But remember, please remember, I'm
here for you; I'll always be here for you." And I
heard, to my right, "You're fooling yourself."

I recognized the voice, though I couldn't see the
man. "Martin?"

He said, "Are you looking for your wife, Mr.
Harris?"

I hesitated, felt anger welling up, fought it back. "What in the hell do you know about Erika?"

"Not very much, my friend. But a bit more than you do, apparently."

I inhaled quickly and deeply in order to keep my anger from building. The air was cool. "If you have something to say to me, perhaps you could come over here and say it." The beam of a flashlight stabbed at me then. I closed my eyes. "Christ, stop that, you idiot!" I hissed. I heard the flashlight click off.

Martin said, "We take care of them from time to time, Mr. Harris." A pause. "They get confused. They come here. And we take care of them."

"Christ, will you make some sense?!"

"Listen to the woman," he said. Then, faintly, I heard footfalls in the tall grass to my right, where his voice had been.

"Martin?" I called. "We're not done here." I listened. I heard nothing. "Martin, goddamnit, I said we're not finished talking here." Silence.

I went back to the house.

Erika and I have talked about having kids. In the first couple of years of our marriage she was very keen on the idea. We discussed names; she proclaimed that she wanted a boy, and I said I wanted a girl, and then we said in unison, "Whatever we get, we'll keep," which made us laugh.

We worked hard for several years at having kids. We put everything we had into it, even to the point that it was becoming a chore (which, we were told later, probably "increased the difficulty due to tension").

Eventually we decided that each of us had to have a thorough checkup. I was first and I was fine—everything worked. Then it was Erika's turn. She was reluctant, needed persuasion, but she had her checkup and everything appeared to be in good working order with her, too. We decided that we were just having bad luck, so we redoubled our efforts.

It did no good. At the end of our fourth year of marriage we had stopped actively trying to have kids.

Two years later we came here, to the farmhouse.

And one day, not long after we'd moved in, she came to me and said, "We're going to have kids, Jack," which I naturally assumed meant she was pregnant. It made me very happy, of course. I threw my arms around her and lifted her—I thought, as I had several times before, that she was awfully light—kissed her, and said "Great!" again and again.

Then she said, "Not that I'm pregnant, Jack. I don't mean I'm pregnant."

I set her down. Maybe she was talking about adopting. I asked her if that's what she meant.

She shook her head. "No. I mean, literally, we're going to have children."

"Oh, it's a kind of wish, is that what you mean? Here we are, set up in our house in an idyllic country setting, so of course, eventually, we're going to have children. Is that what you're talking about?"

"Sure." But she seemed unconvinced.

"That's not what you mean, is it?" She was confusing me.

She shook her head again. "I don't think so, Jack. I'm sorry if I've misled you. I think what I mean is"—a short, happy smile—"we're going to have kids," and her tone was precisely what it was when she'd said it the first time, as if she were making a surprise announcement, but one that was a surprise to her, too.

"*Who's* going to have kids, Erika?"

We were outside, in front of the house. I had my Nikon in hand because I was taking some pictures of the house. She held her arms wide, did a quick, graceful pirouette, and said, "*We* are!"

I got the distinct impression that "we" had nothing to do with me, which made me nervous and confused.

I reached out, tickled her at the waist; she's always been outrageously ticklish. She let her arms fall, stood quietly for a moment under the big window at the front of the house; I took a picture of her there, a Mona Lisa smile on her mouth.

"*We're* going to have kids, Jack," she said after the shutter clicked. "*We're* going to have kids."

CHAPTER TWO

When I was twelve years old, I was walking the shores of Irondequoit Bay, near Rochester, New York, and I came upon the bloated carcass of a German shepherd that had apparently drowned several weeks earlier. I remember that I stood for a couple of minutes, several feet from it, staring at it. I didn't let my eyes wander over the body; I concentrated only on an area near the bottom of the ribcage, where there was a small, cream-colored hole. Someone had been poking the body there with a pointed stick. The stick lay nearby. After a couple of minutes I took a step forward, hesitated, took another step, picked the stick up—saw some fur clinging to the end of it—and then prodded the body with it. I poked at its belly. I think that somewhere inside me I expected that because it was so bloated, it might explode, and I thought that would be a terrific thing to see.

I had two dogs, myself, then. I had an Irish setter and a black-and-white mongrel, and I loved them. What I was poking at didn't seem to be the same sort of creature. This creature was dead, most importantly. If it had once had a master who loved it and fed it and let it curl up at his feet, that was all behind it now. And it didn't *look* very much like a dog, either. It looked like the fat and grisly caricature of a dog. If I'd encountered it on the street just after it had been killed by a car, I would have had different feelings about it. Maybe I would have wept for it, stroked it.

I poked it with the stick for a good long time. I never got up the nerve to poke it hard enough to put a hole in it, and I envied whoever had been able to put that first hole in it. After a while I got tired of this game, threw the stick into the bay, and started to make my way around the body. I stopped. I had looked at the face before, of course, but now I studied it. The eyes were open and the tongue—big and white and bloated—filled its mouth. I thought that if I waited for a while, it would at last look like a dog and I'd feel sorry for it. That didn't happen. It was still just the fat caricature of a dog.

I had my first nightmare about the dog several

nights later. I continued having nightmares about it
for years.

It was a lot less tidy around Martin's house than I
had imagined it would be. What I'd seen of it from
the road had suggested money, which suggested
neatness, but I was wrong.

A yellow Arctic Cat snowmobile stood near the
house, to the right of the wide wraparound porch. Its
hood was open; various tools were on the seat, and
its right-hand tread lay behind it in the mud. A red
Bombardier Skidoo, intact except for a missing
headlight, stood at right angles to the Arctic Cat, as
if someone had pulled up there to help out.

Another red Bombardier Skidoo—orange flames
painted on the engine cowling—lay on its side twenty
feet away, near a four-car garage. Snowmobile parts
were everywhere around the garage—hoods, seats,
engine parts, treads. Some of the smaller parts had
been trampled into the mud by footfalls.

A battered and rusty Jeep CJ-5 was in the rear
section of the garage, its right front tire gone, the
axle up on cinder blocks. An ancient Dodge Dart,
apparently in the process of being restored, stood
next to it. Its driver's door was open wide, its hood
up; a thermos bottle lay on its side near the left front
tire—what looked like coffee had pooled around it.

Two overhead fluorescent shop lights were burning.
The one above the Dart flickered occasionally.

It was clear that lots of things had been eaten in
the garage: Frito's Corn Chips and Schweppes Gin-

ger Ale, curd cheese, Snickers bars, Genesee Light
Beer. Wrappers, cartons, and bottles littered the place.
Like the snowmobile parts, they had been trampled
underfoot, too.

Footprints were everywhere. The prints of boots
and shoes, even the prints of small, naked feet.

There was a woman in the driver's seat of the
Dart. I saw her first at an angle, from behind. She
was wearing a dark blue dress with a delicate white
flower print on it, and it was this dress and her calves
and bare feet that I saw first. Her left arm hung at her
side, fingers curled. I could see the side of her head,
a mass of brown curls, a long, gently muscled neck.
I said, "Hello?"—although I believe I realized at
once that she was dead. "Hello," I repeated, then
added, "Are you all right?" Something inside me—
some comedian who's inside all of us and who sur-
faces at such times solely to keep us sane—said, "Of
course she's not all right, asshole. She's dead!" I
took a couple of steps to my left, so I could get a
better look at her and keep her at a distance at the
same time. "Are you all right?" I said yet again.
The phrase gave me a little comfort somehow. "Do
you need help?" I added. "Can I give you some
help?" Martin's words—"You're fooling yourself"—
came back to me.

I took a step into the garage then, closer to the
woman in the Dart. "Huh?" I said to her, which was
an extension of my question, "Are you all right?"

"Huh?" *Are you all right?* "Huh?" *Honey,* said
the comedian.

The dress she was wearing was short-sleeved, puffed at the shoulders, 1940's-style, and her skin was dark, as if she had a good, even tan. "What are you doing there?" I asked her. Her head was tilted slightly to her right, and her right arm was on the back of the seat, as if she were in the process of putting her head to the side to rest. But her head had stopped halfway.

I was close enough now to see that there were keys in the ignition. "Were you going somewhere?" I asked and felt foolish saying it because I could dimly see the reflection of her face in the windshield and I could see that her mouth was open slightly; her eyes, too. I could see, also, that she looked quite a lot like Erika. I thought she was Erika, in fact, and I panicked. I ran to her, leaned over into the car, put my hands on her shoulders, started babbling at her, "Erika, oh my God, Erika," again and again. I stopped when I saw that the woman was not Erika. I backed out of the car, hit my head on the top of the door frame, backed away further, into the Jeep CJ-5. I saw myself doing all this and I thought it was comical in a grim way, a very grim and slapstick sort of way, so of course, I started laughing. I heard myself laughing and through it I said to myself, "Stop it, goddamnit!" several times, until I finally did stop.

The woman in the Dart had fallen over in the seat. I came forward and reached into the car, as if I intended to sit her up again. But I backed away. Squeamishness, I think. Mundane and reasonable squeamishness. I muttered to myself something about good sanitary habits, and it brought a small, self-amused grin to my lips. I fought the grin back, reached to my left, took hold of the car door, leaned over again. The Dart was a two-door and I saw that the other door was locked. I locked the driver's door, closed it gently, tried it. It wouldn't open. I smiled and nodded, congratulating myself for my presence of mind. No one would have an opportunity to tamper with the body until the authorities arrived.

Martin's house stood on what was apparently a man-made plateau jutting out of the side of the mountain. Nothing had been planted on this plateau except grass, and it was in sore need of cutting; it crowded up to the sides of the garage and the gravel driveway, and had all but overgrown several field-stone walkways.

I heard rock music coming from inside the house as I approached it, an old Blood, Sweat, and Tears recording, "God Bless the Child," and I listened to it a moment.

It wasn't piercingly loud, but it was loud enough that I'd have to knock very hard. I didn't want to do that. I wanted to knock softly because the thing I had to say was very somber—"I'm afraid there's a dead woman in the car in the garage"—a thing that required quiet and thoughtfulness and tact.

I was twenty feet or so from the house when these thoughts came to me. In hindsight I realize that the reality of the situation was almost cloying—I see the snowmobile parts lying about, the remains of quick lunches trampled underfoot, I smell the faint and unmistakable odor of the cedar logs that the house was made of, I hear "God Bless the Child," I feel the brisk, chill air. And I think how terribly *motionless* it all was, as if it were some gritty and depressing piece of art I'd gotten caught in.

The music stopped abruptly, before the end of the song. I said to myself, *It'll start again*, so I yelled, "Hello? Martin?" I waited for an answer, got none, took a few steps closer to the house, stopped again. "Martin? It's Jack Harris, your neighbor from across the road." The music started at the point it had ended—"God bless the child who can/stand on his own"—and I cursed, glanced back at the garage, at the Dart, at the litter, at the snowmobile parts, the winking shop light, the footprints everywhere. "Martin?" I yelled louder, to be heard above the music—"God bless the child who can/stand up and say/'I've got my own . . .' "—"Martin, it's Jack Harris from across the road." I wanted to go back to my house. The woman in the Dart was none of my business. Erika was my business. I wanted to go back to the house and wait for her.

The music stopped. I stared dumbly at the house for a moment, called "Martin?" again softly, hesitated at the bottom of the steps, climbed them, crossed the porch to the front door, knocked. "Hello?" I said.

The door was made of cedar, like the house itself, and had a small, round window in it. I stood on my tiptoes, peered through this window, through the lace curtain on the inside, at what I supposed was the living room.

I heard rifle fire from well behind me. Across the road, I thought, and to the south.

The second time I lost track of Erika it was several weeks before my accident. We were on another walking tour of our property, had wandered wherever our feet wanted to take us, and they had taken us north, down the wide grassy path that had once been Goat's Head Road, then to the dismal log cabin that sat close to the path. We began discussing again the idea of burning it down. To my surprise, Erika's feelings about that had changed. She didn't want to burn it down; she wanted to leave it just as it was.

"Why?" I asked.

"For anyone who might need it," she answered.

"Who, for instance?" I paused. "Whom," I corrected.

"Me," she answered.

We had been standing in front of it; I'd been leaning this way and that to look into a small, bare window, *sans* glass, in the front. The place intrigued me. I'd wondered more than once who might have lived in it. Clearly, someone had.

Its front door was open, hanging inward. Erika went to it, through several yards of stunted quack grass, and walked in.

I called to her, "Don't go in there, Erika. For God's sake—"

She called back, "I already am in, Jack."

I grimaced. I felt certain that the place was alive with insects and spiders and snakes—perhaps even a rattlesnake or two—and I didn't care for the idea of walking through it.

"Be careful, Erika."

"I'm always careful, Jack."

I waited outside that cabin for several minutes. I heard Erika moving about inside it, heard her say, several times, soothingly, "Oh, hello," and I assumed that she'd found a chipmunk, or a mole.

"Why don't you come out now, Erika?!" I called at last.

"Yes," she called back, "in a minute."

So I waited a minute and called to her again. I got no answer. I called again, "Erika? Are you in there?" Nothing.

I screwed my courage up and went inside.

The walls were fashioned from bare logs; no attempt had been made at plastering them. Here and there, wide cracks between the logs let sunlight in, so there was a random, horizontal crisscross pattern of yellowish light on the north and east walls, and near-total darkness on the south wall. A short doorway led into the back room, and the random pattern of light made a sharp downturn there because the door was partway open.

I stood at the center of the front room and called for Erika again. No answer. I called once more and heard, faintly, as if she were speaking from a room well removed from the one I was in, "Oh, hello."

"Erika, stop playing games."

"Oh, hello." It was closer, just to my right, near the south wall. I looked. I saw nothing.

"Erika?"

"Hello there." Closer still. I took a step forward, toward the south wall.

The floor of the cabin is smooth, hard earth. And as I looked at the dark south wall, I saw Erika rise up, in the corner, and I assumed she'd been crouching there. I said, "Erika, my God, what have you been doing?"

She stepped closer to me so her face and body were in the crisscross pattern of sunlight coming through the front wall. She held her hand out; there was a very small mole in it. She said, "Don't be angry, Jack. I've just been talking to a friend."

CHAPTER THREE

The German shepherd I found on the shore of Irondequoit Bay twenty years ago is still there, unless some civic-minded citizen instituted a cleanup of the bay; if so, the carcass languishes in a landfill somewhere. And I think it's safe to say that there's not much left of it. The skeleton doubtless remains intact. Under the right conditions, it could remain intact for several million years. But the soft stuff— the muscle, the intestines, the skin and cartilage, the eyes and the tongue, the brain, the ligaments, the glands—all has been recalled, has broken down, and been pulled back into the earth. And someday the earth will put the puzzle back together. Another German shepherd will appear. Or maybe a mole. Or an azalea. Or a woman with blue eyes and dark skin whose life will come to its end in a Dodge Dart.

I saw a man through the lace curtains, in Martin's living room. He was sitting in a soiled white club chair, facing me, his head thrown back so the back of his neck was resting on the back of the chair; his mouth was open slightly. He was wearing dark pants and a short-sleeved white shirt, and his bare feet were together, knees parted. He was a young man, I guessed, in his early twenties. He appeared to be very pale, so it was easy to see that there were jagged, dark areas where his skin touched the chair, at his elbows and forearms, for instance, and around his bare feet. These jagged, dark areas grew very slowly as I watched, as if mud were covering him from where his skin touched the chair and the floor; this darkness stained the skin, retreated, stained it again, higher, retreated. I rationalized this at first. I said to myself that I wasn't really *seeing* it. I said to myself that since I couldn't explain it, then *of course* I wasn't seeing it. It was one of the laws of magic—*If you think you're seeing the impossible, then of course you aren't*. I told myself that I was seeing only the room, the soiled white club chair, the man's shoes— Wallabees—next to it, blue socks stuffed inside. I was seeing nothing magical or impossible. Only more remains of lousy lunches—candy wrappers, ginger

ale cans, empty bottles of Genesee Light Beer. And
the body of a young man sat in the midst of it. Like a
totem. *To life!* it said, *This is life!* it said.

But the dark areas were not just dark areas. They
were areas of decay where the skin and tissues were
breaking down very rapidly, like sand sculptures being
broken down by tides.

That's when I turned and ran back to my house.

And found there, at the front door, John, the man
who claimed to have shot a woman several weeks
before. He was standing with his shotgun held diago-
nally across his chest, barrel pointing upward. He
had a wide grin on his mouth.

"Good Christ!" I managed; the run from Martin's
house had left me breathless. I hadn't seen John until
I'd rounded the privet hedge.

"Hi," he said.

I cursed again, stopped a good fifty feet from him.
"What are you doing here, John?"

He nodded once at the shotgun. "I got it loaded,
Mr. Harris."

I stared silently at him for half a minute. Then I
started walking very slowly toward him. When I was
within twenty-five feet of him, I held my hand out.
"Why don't you give me the gun, John? Please."

"And I shot someone, too. I really did."

"Did you, now?"

"I did. I shot a man this time." He lifted his chin
toward the north. "Over there. I shot a man because
he was trespassing. I didn't shoot a woman; I shot a
man."

"What man?"

"I don't know. A man who was trespassing." He held the shotgun out to me. "Take it. Go ahead. It ain't loaded. It was loaded, but it ain't no more."

I stepped forward, took the shotgun from him. "Show me the man you shot, John."

He nodded. "Okay. Careful of the mud this time, though. Don't want you gettin' stuck again."

He took me down the wide grassy path that had once been Old Hunt's Hollow Road. We walked for five minutes, no longer, then he stopped and nodded to his right, into the woods. "There he is, Mr. Harris."

I looked. I saw a pair of blue jeans, a brown tweed jacket in the weeds. John saw it, too, and he chuckled. "Must be a *naked* man now, Mr. Harris—this man I shot. Must be a naked *dead* man, now."

And from behind us I heard, "What's in there?" The words were like a sudden pain, sharp and quick; a small grunt of surprise came out of me. Again I heard, "What's in there?" Then: "What do you think you're seeing in there, Mr. Harris?"

I turned my head. Martin stood several feet away. He had his hands shoved casually into the pockets of his blue jeans, and when he said "What's in there?" again, he nodded toward the blue jeans and the brown tweed jacket as if we were merely out window-shopping and he was asking about a display of luggage.

A low curse came out of me.

"Don't swear at me, Mr. Harris. Just tell me what you see in there."

I shook my head in confusion. "I don't know."

He stepped forward slowly, hesitated, lifted his head again. "What do you *think* you're seeing there?"

And I answered simply, "A man who has died."

"But there is no man there, Mr. Harris. So that's not what you're seeing at all. You must realize that by now." He stuck his hands into his pockets again. "This is where they come. Some of them. To this place. Because this is where they were born."

"That's insane," I said. "Obviously, this lunatic here"—I indicated John—"has actually shot someone this time, and it has nothing at all to do with these creatures you've conjured up."

"I didn't conjure them up. The earth did. The earth"—he took his right hand from his pocket, made quotes with his fingers—" 'conjured them up.' Just like your mother and father conjured you up. And now these creatures, these *people,* Mr. Harris, are going *back* to the earth. It's all very, very simple. They're going back *into* the earth."

I looked silently at him for several seconds. I sighed. "I'm going to call the police. I'm going to call what's-his-name . . ."

"Larry Whipple?"

"Yes. I'm going to go back to my house now, I'm going to call him and I'm going to tell him what's happened here."

"Of course you are."

I started backing away, turned, stopped.

Martin said, "You do have my sympathies, Mr. Harris. These people are very easy to love." And he grinned.

I was close to him, within arm's reach.

He added, "It's just too bad they don't *last* longer, isn't it?" His grin broadened.

I dropped the shotgun. I didn't hit Martin with my fist. As a teenager, I'd made that mistake. I'd challenged the school bully, had seen a quick and lucky opening, and had hit him square in the cheekbone with my clenched fist. I'd broken his cheekbone, and three of my knuckles as well.

I hit Martin with an open hand so my palm landed just on the left side of his nose. I felt his nose crumble, and for an instant I experienced immense, almost numbing satisfaction. Then he fell backwards. His hand went to his nose, and a low snuffling sound came from him, like the noise a pig makes. Even before he hit the ground, I was apologizing to him. "Jesus, I'm sorry, my God—"

He hit the ground, sat for an instant, then thudded backwards, hand still at his nose. An "Uh!" came out of him, followed by a muffled "Fuck!"

I stepped forward, reached to help him up, straightened. Nearby, John said, "Hey, good one."

"Yes," I whispered, "wasn't it?" And I walked quickly back to my house and locked the doors.

The house was cold, the kind of cold that slides over the skin and pushes into the pores. It even smelled cold, like a freezer that needs defrosting. I went into the dining room, turned the thermostat up, heard the furnace kick on, felt momentarily grateful for that small distraction.

"Jack?" I heard distantly, from the second floor. "Is that you?" It was Erika's voice. "It's your turn to cook tonight, Jack."

CHAPTER FOUR

She was at the top of the stairs. She was wearing blue jeans, a cream-colored long-sleeved blouse, the wristwatch I'd bought her for Christmas three years earlier. And when I looked at her from the bottom of the stairs, she smiled and said again, "It's your turn to make supper tonight, Jack." It was well lighted there, where she was standing. I could see that the left-hand sleeve of her blouse was unbuttoned; it caught my eye because she was holding that arm up, elbow bent, and she was idly rubbing her cheek.

I said her name of course, a low and incredulous

whisper, and she cocked her head to the right, looked bemused, and asked, "What's wrong, Jack?" She noticed her blouse was unbuttoned then, and began buttoning it with her right hand. "I'll be down in a few minutes." She disappeared into the bedroom.

I screamed her name. Once. Then again, halfway up the stairs, and again, softer, as I entered the bedroom. I was aware that a quivering, disbelieving smile was on my lips. "Erika?" I hesitated, said it again, "Erika," glanced about, saw the rocking chair, the unmade bed, the tall, dark chest of drawers. "Erika?" I said once more. I looked into the open closet; I stepped into it. "Erika?" I swept my arm into the clothes hanging there, said loudly, "Erika?" I swept the clothes to the floor; I screamed, "Erika!"

It was several hours before I left the bedroom. I spent some time mumbling her name. I spent some time hunched forward in the rocking chair, my fists clenched in front of me, my head down. And I spent some time weeping, a lot of time weeping. Then I sat back in the chair, put my head back, and whispered her name. I wasn't calling to her anymore; I was admitting how much a part of me she was and how much a part of the house she was. At last, mid-afternoon sunlight broke into the room and I pushed myself out of the chair and went downstairs to prepare the dinner. I found spinach and garlic pasta in the cupboard, which pleased me, and a large can of Italian-style tomato paste, which makes an excellent sauce. The house had warmed up considerably, so I turned the thermostat down. I hesitated, went to the stairway, and called tentatively, "Erika?" waited a moment, got no reply, went into the kitchen and made a lavish dinner. I prepared the table lovingly. I set two places, of course. I put some daffodils that I'd found just outside the kitchen door in a vase in the center of the table. I put candles on the table, too, on either side of the vase, and lit them. I ladled out the pasta, the sauce, the salad. I stepped back, congratulated myself. Then I turned my head slightly. "It's ready, Erika," I called

And I sat. And waited.

She loved the meals I prepared, was always on time for them, so there was a clear purpose in waiting, but even as I waited (and I waited a long time—until the pasta got cold and the salad went limp), I asked myself if I was really doing something rational. I supposed that I wasn't. I supposed that I was merely putting time off, that waiting at the dinner table was a kind of *timeless* thing.

But I wasn't sure I wanted her to come to dinner. I didn't know who she was; she was playing games. She'd played games with Will, and now she was playing them with me, and I started asking myself just how she'd conned me into sharing my life with her.

I even said at one point while I waited, "Goddamnit, Erika, will you cut the horsing around?!"

She did not come to dinner. I ate both plates of cold pasta, both limp salads, snuffed out the candles, and went into the living room to sleep.

It was dusk, almost 7:00. The big window in the living room faced west, so the view I had from the couch was warm and comforting. I said to myself, "There can be no trouble on a day that ends like this." It was simple and untrue, and it wrapped me up and made me feel good.

"Are you in the house, Erika?" I said. "*Where* are you? Are you hiding? Don't hide. Come down; we'll talk." I paused. "I want to know you, I need to know you."

The view I had out that window was panoramic. It took in the front yard, the road, all of the mountain beyond. I could see the path that led to Martin's house, too, and I could see someone on it, a man, I supposed, because of the way he walked—arms swinging casually, legs stiff. He wore dark pants and a short-sleeved white shirt. It didn't come to me that it was the young man I'd seen in Martin's living room until he had reached my driveway and had started up it.

We have a number of spotlights on the house. When they're all burning, the place looks like a carnival.

The young man was partway up the driveway when I switched the front light on. It seemed to take him by surprise. He held his arm up to shield his eyes and I could see that there wasn't much left of his arm, only half of it perhaps, laterally, down its length. Then he put his arm down and I watched as he made his way to the front storm door. I heard him push on it several times. I heard it open, heard him walk across the porch, knock on the front door.

I called, "What do you want?"

"Hello?" he called.

"What do you *want*?" I repeated.

"Is someone home?" He knocked again.

"Go away!"

"Could I talk to someone, please? Is someone home? I need to talk to someone."

I said nothing. I went to the window that looks out on the porch, bent over, looked through a space in the inside shutters. He was in partial darkness on the porch. The spotlight was illuminating the back of his shirt, some of the back of his head. I saw his arm go up, saw him knock again. "Is someone in the house, please? Could I talk to someone in the house?"

I called spontaneously, surprising myself, my gaze still on him, "What are you doing here?"

He turned his head so the spotlight lit the side of his face; he saw me, called back, "Oh," as if surprised. "Hi. Am I bothering you? Could I talk to you? Could I talk to someone in the house?" He smiled. "I need to talk to someone in the house." It was not a good smile. Much of the side of his face was gone, in a ragged vertical line from the middle of his cheek to what had once been the back of his head. Without that, his smile would have been pleas-

ant and good-natured, and I thought that lots of doors
had been probably coaxed open by it.

"No," I said, my voice low.

His smile increased, so the edge of it was lost in
the darkness at the side of his head. "I have an offer
for you, Mr. . . . Mr. . . ."

"Please," I said, my voice still low. I couldn't
bring it up much past the level of a whisper. "Go
away."

"I have an offer for you. I have an offer for you,
sir."

I was stuck on that spot, of course, at the window,
and I could feel that I was starting to hyperventilate; I
forced myself to take a long, slow breath.

The young man rattled on, "I have an offer for
you, sir."

"Do you?" I whispered.

"Sorry?" he said.

"Do you?" I repeated.

"I do. I have an offer for you. Open the door,
please." I saw movement behind him, between the
porch and the little stream to the south of the house—a
slow and graceful kind of movement that came and
went quickly. "I have an offer for you, sir." His
voice was high-pitched, and scarred, as if his vocal
cords were in the process of shredding.

I yelled at him, "Get out of here, goddamnit;
get off my property—I don't want you here!"

Someone was singing to the south of the house.
An aria from *Carmen*.

"Land is your best investment, sir," said the young man on the porch. His voice sounded very bad now. It sounded like sheet metal being torn.

"Nothing is quite so precious as the land, sir. It nourishes us, gives us pleasure, so why don't we grab a *piece* of it, sir." He paused meaningfully. "I represent Dominion Properties, of Colorado, sir. My card." He put his fingers into his shirt pocket, brought them out, empty, held them up. "My card." He smiled yet again, but the edge of his smile was gone now; it had vanished into the darkness that was pushing forward from the back of his head, up his arms and his legs. He put his fingers back into his shirt pocket. His smile vanished. He took his fingers from his pockets, turned back to the door, knocked on it. "I would like to speak to someone in the house," he called. "I need to speak . . ." His voice stopped. His lips continued moving, but his voice stopped, and I could see that jagged darkness overtaking him.

Sarah said, *They sprang from the earth, Jack. Like the trees did. And the mushrooms. And the azaleas.*

The earth conjured them up, Martin said. *Just like your mother and father conjured you up. And now they are going back to the earth. It's all very simple. They're going back into the earth.*

I stepped away from the window. I heard quick shuffling noises on the porch. I whispered, "Go away! Damnit, go away!" The shuffling noises stopped. I heard distantly, to the south of the house, bits and pieces of *Carmen,* and from above, from the bedroom Erika and I shared, I heard someone moving about quickly and fitfully.

I remember pulling the front door open. I remember hesitating on the porch, though very briefly, just long enough to see that the young man had backed himself into a corner where Erika kept a rake, a shovel, a large bag of grass seed, and I could see that he had fallen there and was sitting on the grass seed. He was in darkness, so I didn't see much, only that he'd raised his hand, that he was trying desperately to pull himself up; I could hear slight, soft brushing noises, too, and I guessed it was his shirt brushing against the aluminum siding behind him.

I remember backing away from him to the screen door. It always stuck when it was opened, and because he had pushed it open, it had stayed open. I remember turning, hesitating again at the top of the porch steps, listening, hearing nothing at all for several moments. "Erika?" I whispered. A car sped past down Hunt's Hollow Road.

"Jack?" I heard. It was Erika's voice.

I muttered several low curses. Then I ran to my Toyota, fumbled for the keys in my pocket, cursed again because I was sitting on them and had to do a number of contortions to get at them.

I turned the ignition key and looked back at the house all in the same breath. I saw a female figure at our window. The bedroom light was on behind her, so all I could see of her was her dark outline against

the light. I rolled my window down. I stared at her
for several seconds. "I love you, Erika, I do love
you," I whispered. "But, my God, you're scaring
the hell out of me."

CHAPTER FIVE

Near the beginning of Hunt's Hollow Road, where it branches to the north and south —Cohocton is south—Knebel flagged me down. He was walking his aged German shepherd, Hans, on a short, black leash, much like the leashes blind people use, and was carrying a small suitcase.

I pulled up next to him, put the parking brake on because I was pointing downhill, and rolled the window down. Knebel leaned over and grinned at me. I recoiled from the odor of the little cigars he smoked.

"Jack," he said, still grinning, "we got trouble in

Cohocton tonight. Got lots of people leaving Cohocton tonight.''

"I have trouble of my own, Knebel," I said. He didn't hear me. I'd said it at a very low whisper.

"I didn't hear you, Jack," he said.

I tried again. "Goddamnit, Knebel," I said, and my voice gurgled higher as I said it, "I've got trouble of my own!"

"Can I get in? We'll talk." He didn't wait for an answer. He went around to the passenger side, opened the door, shooed Hans into the backseat, and got into the front, with his suitcase on his lap. He was still grinning. "People," he said, "standing by themselves, in the dark." He lifted his hands, swept them wide; his right hand hit the passenger window. "*Every*where, Jack." I heard Hans groaning in the backseat. "Everywhere," he repeated, and swept his arms wide again, hit the window once more; a little "Ouch!" came from him. He held his fingers up close to his face. "Turn the light on, Jack." I turned the overhead light on. He studied his fingers a moment, glanced around at Hans, said, "No, Hans, not now!" and looked at me again. "Jack," he began.

I cut in, "I don't have time for you tonight, Knebel."

His grin reappeared. "No one's got time for Knebel, and I understand that. Knebel's old, and Knebel's feeble"—his grin strengthened—"and Knebel's not playing with a full deck, as the saying goes, but this time Knebel *knows*, and I'll tell you what Knebel knows—"

I reached past him and pushed the door open. "Out," I said. "I don't have time for you tonight; I have problems of my own."

His grin vanished. "I'll tell you what Knebel knows, Jack. He knows that there's trouble in Cohocton tonight, and so he's getting out. Lots of people are getting out. Because the trouble's just started." He got out of the car, leaned over, pushed the seat forward. "C'mon, Hans," he said. Hans had been licking himself; he continued licking himself. "C'mon, Hans!" Knebel said again, more forcefully, reached in, grabbed Hans's leash, and yanked hard on it. A little squeal came from Hans, and he reluctantly got out of the car. Knebel slammed the door. I took the emergency brake off. Knebel leaned over. "Hey, Jack?"

I looked at him. "Yes?"

He gave me the finger, quick and hard. "Fuck you, Jack!"

I drove to the bottom of the hill and turned north, away from the center of Cohocton.

I saw a man jogging soon after I made the turn. I had seen him before. I had even stopped to talk to him once. He wore yellow running shorts tonight, a white T-shirt, blue sneakers, and as I passed him I glanced quickly at him. I saw that much of his face was gone and most of his chest, too, I guessed, because the T-shirt described a large and ragged pit there. And as I glanced at him I saw a young woman in a long coat leave her house, a little blonde girl beside her, also dressed in a long coat. The young woman saw the jogger and stood bolt upright, put her arm around the little girl, then hurried her toward an ancient Ford wagon parked in the driveway.

I stopped the car, looked back. I saw the jogger stumble, saw him fall face first, saw him try pathetically to push himself up in the roadway.

And beyond him, in the village, dozens of people were hurrying stiffly from place to place, from the bank to one of the five hardware stores, to that bizarre little clothing store, to their cars, from here to there and back again, without so much as a nod to one another, as if they were doing something that was necessary, even desperately necessary, but very unpleasant, too.

I saw the woman and little girl get into the Ford; I saw it back out of the driveway.

And I saw the jogger give one great heave upward with his arms, get himself up several inches, pause, push again, get himself up another few inches. And collapse. I looked away.

Moments later the Ford roared past me, out of Cohocton.

I sat quietly in the car for several minutes, my hands hard on the wheel, my head shaking nervously. The dusk turned quickly to darkness, and when I glanced in the rearview mirror, I saw a slight black swelling in the road where the jogger's body was. Beyond it, in the village—lighted by a half-dozen yellow street lamps—I saw that people still were coming and going very quickly, very purposefully, some with their heads down. I turned back. Several hundred feet in front of me, at an IGA store Erika and I used, people carried bags of groceries to their cars, then went back for more.

I heard the wail of Cohocton's volunteer ambulance after a few moments. In the rearview mirror the ambulance's pulsating red light appeared distantly. I watched as the ambulance approached the spot where the jogger's body was, then slowed, the siren winding down like a top. That's when Knebel tapped on my window with the end of Hans's leash and scared the hell out of me.

"Jesus!" I reached over, opened the door.

He did as he'd done before. He shooed Hans into the backseat, climbed into the front, grinned. "You been watchin' what's been goin' on here, Jack?"

"Christ," I said.

"Yes, you have. I can tell." He nodded backwards to indicate the town. "And you been watchin' what's goin' on there, have ya?"

"Yes," I managed.

He nodded sagely. "Some of these people around here are nuts, Jack, though I guess you figured that out for yourself. But they're not so nuts that they're gonna try and share their town with a bunch of spooks." He let out a grisly little chuckle. "Know how long I been here, Jack? I been here, in Cohocton, for fifty-five years. And that's a long damned time to be in one damned place, believe me; long enough, in fact, to see lots of things come and go. And come again." He turned in the seat, looked out the back window. I looked in the rearview mirror. In the lights from the ambulance, the body of the jogger—what was left of it—was being put on a stretcher. "Like that one there," Knebel said.

"I don't understand."

"Like that one there," he repeated. "Like that jogger. He's been here before."

I nodded grimly. "Yes. I know. I've seen him a couple of times."

Knebel shook his head. "That's not what I mean, Jack. That's not what I mean at all. I mean, I seen him ten *years* ago, and I seen him *twenty* years ago, and I seen him *thirty* years ago."

The ambulance turned its siren on once more, made a wide U-turn, headed back the way it had come.

"Along with some of the others. Like your wife. They come and they go; they come and they go."

"What in the hell are you talking about, Knebel?"

"Just what I said. They come and they go. They pop up and they go back and they pop up again, pretty much the same as they were before. The same as us."

"You're not making any sense."

"Sure I am." He glanced back at Hans. "Stop that, Hans. Later." He looked at me. "What am I, Jack? Tell me what I am."

"I don't know what you're talking about, Knebel."

"I'll tell you what I am. I'm an old man. I'm tall and I'm pale and I have an old dog and people think I'm not all there. My God, Jack, there are a thousand men just like me alive right now. Line us up together, and you'd have to get real close to tell us apart. But then there's the people like your wife, like that jogger and the rest of 'em. The people out there standing by themselves in the dark. They're like palmettos, Jack. They're like chips of quartz, or leaves, or moles. They come and they go and who knows who's who, Jack? No one.''

"For Christ's sake, Knebel, this doesn't have a damned thing to do with Erika.''

"Oh, but it does, Jack. It does. Go on home and see for yourself.'' He nodded. "Go and find out for yourself. Look hard.'' Then he opened his door, got Hans out, and was gone.

CHAPTER SIX

I remember that Erika went through a period of a couple of weeks, maybe a month, when she hated the color of her hair, so she had it dyed dark blonde. Whoever dyed it did a bad job, though. It was streaked with her own very dark brown, and the roots were brown, but since it seemed to please her, I said nothing. She didn't let on until much later that she had seriously considered having it redyed because she *knew* how bad the job was and she thought she looked like a clown. But she'd made a decision, had been firm about it, and so the dye job stayed until she thought the time was right to announce that her natural hair color was okay. It was a thoroughly human thing to do, an imperfect and endearing thing to do.

I turned and drove into Cohocton. I stopped, got out.

I saw the people standing, as Knebel had said, "by themselves in the dark."

Some were like faded paintings on the walls of the village, and some were like the fainter of two shadows cast by two lights, and some still were whole, and some that were whole were weeping, and some were whispering harshly, and some were whispering very softly, and some were talking out loud.

"I can't help you if you won't help yourself," said one.

"Yes, of course," said another, "I'll throw a Tupperware party."

And from another: "The lessons begin on Friday? How much are they, please?"

And: "The damned train is late again."

And: "That was nice; that was *very* nice."

"Cloudy tomorrow, with a chance of rain."

"In our discussion of phobias, we must first *define* the term."

"Why did she do it, Daddy?"

Vivid approximations of humanity winding down.

Darkness had come by then, but the street lamps were good and the town was well lighted.

Jean, the thirtyish, matronly postmistress, was coming out of the drugstore with a bag in her arm: "Pharmaceuticals; I need lots of pharmaceuticals," she told me, though I hadn't asked. She was near her car, an old Chrysler New Yorker she'd parked in front of the drugstore. She opened the rear door, tossed the bag in, slammed the door, and turned back to me. "You're Mr. Harris, aren't you?"

"Yes."

"What are you doing here, Mr. Harris?"

I shook my head.

She glanced very quickly to my right. I looked. I saw the dark suggestion of a man there, several yards away, in the narrow passage between the drugstore and the building beside it. He appeared to be standing with his back against the wall of the drugstore; he seemed to be holding his hands to the sides of his head.

I glanced back at Jean, and she at me. I asked her, "Who are these people, Jean?"

"What people?" she said. She repeated, "What people?"—then got into the New Yorker, slammed the door, rolled her window down. "Go back home, Mr. Harris. Everyone belongs at home tonight." She started the car and sped off.

I glanced again at the man in the passageway. He was down on his knees, hands still at his head. I said to him, "Can I help you; do you need help?"

And he was gone.

"She's right," I heard from behind me.

I turned. Larry Whipple was at the other side of the street. John stood next to him.

"Home's the best place for us all tonight, Mr. Harris," Whipple added.

I pointed at the passageway. "There's a man here who needs help."

"No, Mr. Harris. You're wrong. Please go home. Get your provisions; get what you need. And then go home. Stay home. Enjoy your home, Mr. Harris. Enjoy it for a couple of days."

I looked again at the passageway. I looked at Larry Whipple. "Please go home, Mr. Harris!" he said.

I saw then that John was carrying the shotgun I'd taken from him at the house. As I watched, he levelled it. I looked again at the passageway. It was empty except for a shadow that moved and shimmered. I looked back at John.

"Christ," I screamed. "What in the fuck are you doing?"

"Get out of the way, Mr. Harris!" Whipple ordered.

"You can't *shoot* him, for God's sake—"

"I'm shooting no one. Now, please, get *out* of the way!"

I shook my head.

John fired.

From behind me, from the passageway, I heard a muted "Uh!" and then a quick thumping sound.

On our third wedding anniversary Erika and I went to Toronto. I'd never been to Toronto, and she said that I hadn't lived until I'd gone up in the CN Tower, which was billed as the "highest observation deck in the world."

"I'm afraid of heights," I told her, which wasn't entirely true. I'm afraid of ladders; I'm afraid of climbing up on roofs. But heights per se merely make me a little nervous. If I'm completely sure of what stands between me and the ground, I can adjust easily to any height.

"Who cares if you're afraid of heights?" she said. "I'll hold your hand."

So we went to Toronto and took the glass-enclosed, external elevator of the CN Tower first to the 1100-foot level, which was interesting but only vaguely dizzying, then climbed into another elevator, at the center of the tower, which took us to the 1450-foot level. That was more like it. It was night, past twelve, when we went up there, and there was a heavy cloud cover, so separating the horizon from the sky was next to impossible.

"We're in a black bubble," I said.

"You're a cynic," she said, then hurried on, "If I jumped, I wonder if they'd *find* anything, Jack. Maybe I'd just, *phump!* mix right up with whatever's down there. If it's clay, I'm clay; if it's asphalt, I'm asphalt. What do you think?"

"I think they'd find parts of you in Schenectady."

What could I do that night in Cohocton? I got back into my Toyota and drove home.

CHAPTER SEVEN

I did look hard for Erika, as Knebel had suggested.
I decided that's the one thing I hadn't done; I hadn't
looked hard—I hadn't looked hard *enough*. So I went
back to the house, and I looked hard, and of course, I
found her.

She was in the bedroom upstairs. AND WE'RE STILL
HERE said the graffito in the closet. She was there,
too. She was in the dining room, and in her music
room; she was in the kitchen; she was in her garden.
She walked with me a while through her garden, and
I talked to her about inconsequentials.

She liked that. She used to complain a lot that I dwelt on heavy philosophical things. So we talked about inconsequentials. About Will, who, I told her, had a very large crush on her, and about Knebel—"He's got your number, kid." And she agreed.

I have photographs of Erika. I take them down when I'm missing her, when her smell has gone and I'm not sure at all where she's gotten off to. And after a while I put them away, because, of course, they're no substitute at all for the real thing. They're only photographs. They cannot touch or breathe or tell me it's my turn to make the dinner.

I'm thankful that Whipple didn't get her. Not that it would have made a whole hell of a lot of difference. I don't think it would have made any difference at all. But I don't like Whipple, and I love Erika. And I despise the fact that the Whipples of this world can so easily get at the Erikas of this world, no matter how necessary it might seem.

Make no mistake. I do not fool myself that she is real, that I can go with her to the sub shop or make love to her or read a book aloud with her into the wee hours. She exists in my memory. She's real in my memory. And our memories do sustain us. They give our present a backdrop, scenery.

At last, they give the earth something to work with. And lately, in the mornings especially, I hear the sounds of children around the house, and I know that the earth is very hard at work, again.